LILY:

A SHORT STORY

STEVIE TURNER

OTHER WORKS
BY STEVIE TURNER

The Pilates Class
A House Without Windows
No Sex Please, I'm Menopausal!
For the Sake of a Child
A Rather Unusual Romance
The Daughter-in-law Syndrome
Revenge
The Noise Effect
The Donor
Cruising Danger
Repent at Leisure
Life: 18 Short Stories
Mind Games
A Marriage of Convenience

Dedicated to all those at the end of their lives.
There but for the grace of God go I.

SYNOPSIS

Lily is 92 and failing in health. Her family tells her she is going on a little holiday, and although she finds herself still on her beloved Isle of Wight, to her horror she is now living permanently in a residential home at the mercy of Bridie, the 'horrible' one.

To make what is left of her life happier she thinks about years gone by, and once again wonders about the strange disappearance of her 14 year old sister Violet in 1897. However, every cloud has a silver lining, and amidst the daily horror of her life she is delighted to find out that somebody at the home can shed new light on the mystery.

Contents

CHAPTER 1 1

CHAPTER 2 4

CHAPTER 3 8

CHAPTER 4 10

CHAPTER 5 13

CHAPTER 6 15

CHAPTER 7 18

CHAPTER 8 20

CHAPTER 9 23

CHAPTER 10 25

CHAPTER 11 27

CHAPTER 12 29

CHAPTER 13 33

CHAPTER 14 35

CHAPTER 15 38

CHAPTER 16 40

CHAPTER 17 42

CHAPTER 18 44

CHAPTER 19 46

CHAPTER 20 48

CHAPTER 21 51

CHAPTER 22 54
CHAPTER 23 56
CHAPTER 24 58
CHAPTER 25 61
CHAPTER 26 63
CHAPTER 27 66
CHAPTER 28 68
CHAPTER 29 71
CHAPTER 30 73
CHAPTER 31 76
CHAPTER 32 78
CHAPTER 33 80
CHAPTER 34 82
CHAPTER 35 84
CHAPTER 36 86
CHAPTER 37 89
CHAPTER 38 92
CHAPTER 39 94
CHAPTER 40 97
CHAPTER 41 100

CHAPTER 1

Lily woke up, looked at her daughter, and opened her mouth to speak.

"Lll …..hrss..pt.."

She could not seem to get the message over to Pamela that she wanted to go home.

"You've had a stroke, Mum. You need to stay in here now so that the nurses can look after you." Pamela plumped up the cushion behind Lily's back and put a cup of water to her lips. "Come on. Have a little drink. There's a sandwich on the table here for you. You've had nothing to eat all the afternoon."

Lily pushed the cup away. If she could not go home, then she wanted to die.

"I'll be back to see you tomorrow. Connie's home from school now, so she'll come with me as well." Pamela kissed her mother. "We'll come after lunch. See you tomorrow!" She tried to sound as cheerful as possible so that her mother's suspicions were not aroused.

With a waft of perfume Pamela was gone. Lily tried to get out of the chair, but her body would not obey her commands. Out of the corner of her eye Lily could see Bridie, the horrible one, coming in. With a few expert moves Lily's clothing was removed and a nightdress put over her head.

"Now, Mrs Read, I'm going to put you on the commode so that you can do a wee for me before I put you into bed."

"Essss.......uurrrrr." Lily tried to say that she wasn't a child, didn't want to do a wee, and didn't want to go to bed.

"You have to do a wee! Your sheets were wet again this morning." Bridie lifted Lily up as though she was a feather, placed the back of her nightdress over the backrest of the commode, and put a blanket over her legs. "I'll come back in a while when you've done a wee."

Lily was stuck fast by her nightdress. She looked around the room in despair. *How could it have come to this? She and Artie had brought six children into the world, looked after them and given them a good life, and now they'd betrayed her. They'd told her she was going on a little holiday. They'd left it to Pamela to dump her here. She would never trust any of her children again.*

***

She felt hungry. Her skinny left arm reached out to her bedside table and grabbed the sandwich still sitting there from tea-time. It tasted good. She wolfed it down, together with a morsel of Madeira cake on the same plate.

If only Artie were alive. He would never have left her here. He would have looked after her. Poor Artie! At the end of his life he wasn't even able to sit on his favourite seat down at Freshwater Bay, and could only look at the windsurfers dancing on the waves through the sitting room window.

Her buttocks were sore by the time the horrible one returned. Rough hands freed her nightdress, and two arms that would not have looked out of place in the wrestling ring grabbed her frail body and moved her onto the bed. She felt her legs being lifted up and thrown down unceremoniously onto the sheet. Two sheepskin heel protectors were attached to her feet. Probing fingers invaded her mouth and removed her teeth. *She wished she'd had the nerve to bite them:*

"I don't want to hear a peep out of you until the morning."

She looked at the clock that for 50 years had taken pride of place on the mantelpiece in her and Artie's front room:

Half past six. Only babies went to bed at half past six!

CHAPTER 2

"Race you to that gorse bush over there!"

Lily tried hard to keep up with her big sister Daisy, but her short legs would not move fast enough. Once again, ten-year-old Daisy had won. Lily looked behind her; their little sister Violet had long ago given up trying to keep up with them, and was walking over High Down alongside their mother, holding her hand.

"I won!"

Daisy's long chestnut hair blew over her face. Her cheeks were rosy in the stiff breeze. Victorious, she threw herself down on the ground, laughing.

"It's not fair!" Lily came along and plonked herself down next to her sister. "Why can't you let me win sometimes?" Her voice came out as a whine.

"I will next time. I promise." Daisy smiled and Lily knew she would. Daisy always kept her promises.

***

"My three little flowers!" Evelyn Roberts found a grassy knoll, sat down with Violet and her two older daughters and opened her capacious bag. "I've got some lunch for all of you and a drink of lemonade before we walk back home."

Lily sat contentedly on the grass nibbling at some bread and cheese. She looked back along the downs the way they had walked:

"Will we see Lord Tennyson today Mama?"

"Maybe we will. Everybody knows he walks along High Down every day." Evelyn sipped her home-made lemonade.

"But he doesn't like seeing people, does he?"

"No Lily, he doesn't. He's had a special door built into the garden of Farringford House so that he can escape from people who wait outside wanting to see him."

"We've learned about Lord Tennyson at school." Violet piped up in her childish voice. "Our teacher read us 'Maud'. It's got my name and Lily's in it, but not Daisy's." Violet stuck her tongue out at her eldest sister and pushed her long flaxen hair away from her face.

"Violet – mind your manners!" Evelyn admonished her daughter and gathered up the leftovers. "It's time to walk home. It's Saturday and Papa will be home early today."

***

Violet complained bitterly on the long walk back as the wind whipped her hair and the downhill slant made her legs ache. All was forgotten though, on reaching the garden gate and catching sight of her father.

Charles Roberts stood in the doorway to greet his family.

"Papa!" Violet flung herself at Charles, who picked up his favourite daughter and spun her around. Violet shrieked with delight.

"You'll make the child dizzy!" Evelyn smiled at her husband.

"There's sweets somewhere in the garden for all my little flowers!" Charles kissed his wife, and watched his daughters fondly as they rushed off to seek the hidden tasty treasures.

"How is Lord Bedbury? Have you heard?" Evelyn gratefully

noticed the full trug of vegetables on the kitchen table.

"He's sinking fast. There'll be a new master of the house before long."

Charles wondered if young Henry was ready to assume the heavy mantle of responsibility.

"Well, he'll still need a head gardener I've no doubt!" Evelyn began peeling the carrots, safe that her husband's position would stay secure. "Let's hope he's as generous to us as Lord Bedbury is."

"Depends if there's any money left when all the gambling and drinking is done. He's well over the age of consent now, so it can't be held in trust." As Charles nibbled on a raw carrot he had a mental image of Lord Henry lying paralytic outside some London whorehouse.

***

"Papa! I found the chocolate beans first! I knew where to find them!" Violet came running to Charles, who had sat himself down in his old worn chair next to the range.

"How did you know where they were, my little princess?"

"I just knew. Can we do some painting today please?" Violet climbed onto her father's lap, the treasured bag of sweets still in her hand.

"Yes. After you share the sweets, we will paint some flowers together." Charles kissed the little girl, who ran off to find her sisters.

"The child has a talent." Charles sucked on his pipe contentedly. "She gets that from you. You could have been an artist."

Evelyn rolled out some pastry, making more noise with the rolling pin than usual:

"And who would cook the dinner while I'm out painting then? My days of sitting down and drawing poppies blowing about in the breeze are over. And who would see to the children?" Evelyn sighed with the unwelcome news she was about to impart: "Before Easter there will be another child. I'm about two months' along."

Charles rose from the chair to hug his wife as she stood at the kitchen table:

"We must thank God for our good fortune."

Evelyn could not share in her husband's delight. All she could see in front of her was more backbreaking, soul-destroying work, and yet another unwanted pregnancy ageing and distorting her once youthful body even more.

CHAPTER 3

"Hey Nana. It's Connie."

"Chchh…." Lily knew quite well who was sitting beside her. *Did they think she was stupid?*

"Don't try and talk." Connie took her grandmother's thin, veined hand and gave it a squeeze. "We've brought you some roses."

Pamela busied herself arranging the flowers in a vase. The wonderful smell from the yellow petals permeated the dreary room, and Lily felt strangely uplifted.

Artie used to bring her red roses on their anniversary.

"Connie's going to start University in October, Mum. She's got a place at Homerton College, Cambridge. She's going to study to become a music teacher." Pamela sounded justifiably proud of her daughter.

Lily could see the family's artistic talent was starting to come out again in a different way in the next generation; her son Edward was a writer and made quite a good living from his novels, and Connie was an excellent pianist and cellist. The arty gene had obviously passed Lily by though, as she had only ever been good at being a mother and looking after her children. Violet had been given the artistic gift but it had gone to waste on the day that Lily would never forget.

***

"We'll pop by tomorrow before we leave. We're going to look around the college, so we'll be staying overnight and catching the ferry back on Saturday morning."

Pamela glanced over at her mother and thought how much more frail she seemed, so silent and somewhat unkempt. However, in the lined face she could see that the light in Lily's grey eyes remained undimmed. She just could not bring herself to tell her mother where else she was going after she had looked around the college.

"Sss…." Lily did not want them to go. *The horrible one would come back in and pin her to the commode again. She was probably waiting outside the door, willing the visitors to leave.*

"It was only a flying visit, just to bring you the roses." Pamela gave Lily a kiss, and her perfume mingled with the smell of the flowers. "We'll be back again soon."

Lily sat there helpless in the chair, resigned to her fate. Footsteps sounded outside in the hallway.

"Hello darling! That was nice – your daughter and granddaughter coming to see you!"

With some effort Lily turned her neck to see who was speaking. *Thank goodness – it was Donna. She was lovely.* Lily breathed a sigh of relief.

"I've put some sugar in it for you." Donna carefully gave Lily a drink of tea from a toddler cup with a lid. Lily tried to smile; she was thirsty and grateful. *The horrible one would never have given her any sugar.*

CHAPTER 4

"Daisy – run to the village please, and get Mrs Lacey. Tell her it's time."

Evelyn could feel the familiar pains beginning. Soon there would be another mouth to feed and no sleep for months. Her breasts would leak and feel uncomfortable. Her husband would be moody at the lack of physical intimacy; her life was not panning out the way she had hoped.

"Lily and Violet; please run to your father and tell him the baby's coming." Evelyn closed her eyes and felt a wave of agony wash over her.

Lily took Violet's hand, and they ran out of their cottage and onto the path leading to Lord Henry's walled garden, where they knew their father would be working. They found him in the greenhouse:

"Hello my little flowers! What brings you here?" Charles diverted his attention from his seedlings to his daughters.

"Mama says the baby's coming." Lily felt safe with her father and did not want to return home without him. She was frightened by her mother's pain.

Charles washed his hands, spoke briefly to his assistant, and prepared to return home. Daisy reappeared shortly afterwards with Mrs Lacey, who always brought the village babies into the world and laid out the dead. Mrs Lacey made her way upstairs to the bedroom, and Charles gathered his daughters together:

"It's a lovely day. I think we should have a little walk down to the bay. We'll leave Mama with Mrs Lacey, and we'll come back again a bit later."

"But I want to stay here with Mama!" Daisy was old enough to realise what was going on.

"Mama doesn't need us all around her now. She has to work hard to bring your little brother or sister into the world." Charles ushered his daughters out of the house and down the road towards Freshwater Bay.

***

Usually Lily would have loved a walk in the sunshine with her father, but today all she wanted to do was to hurry home and see the baby. They had all been out for so long, and had even had dinner in a restaurant. At last though, her father had informed them that it was time to return.

The house seemed too quiet as Charles closed the front door behind them:

"I'll just make sure Mama is awake, and then you can see her."

Charles went quietly upstairs. Lily and her sisters sat on the bottom step, impatiently waiting their turn. Some considerable time passed and he did not reappear. Lily gazed upwards, willing her father to come down.

"I can hear the baby crying! I want to see Mama!" Violet sucked her thumb and began to climb the stairs.

"Come back! There's no baby crying! Papa told us to wait!" Daisy hissed. Violet took no heed of her sister and reached the bedroom door.

Charles, hearing his younger daughter outside the room, came outside:

"Mama is asleep. We must go downstairs."

He took Violet's hand and the girls followed him into the sitting room. He lit the evening lamps, and the room was soon bathed in a soft amber glow. He indicated for his daughters to sit together on the sofa. He sat himself in-between Daisy and Lily, and placed Violet on his lap. He put his arms around the two eldest girls:

"The baby was a boy, but did not survive. He was not born alive. We must help Mama until she is well again." Charles wiped away a stray tear that ran down his cheek and looked at the girls, who gazed back at him in stunned silence.

"I heard him crying!" Violet put her head against her father's shoulder and wept.

"You must have imagined it, child. He never made a sound."

"Can't we see Mama?" Lily cried bitter tears of disappointment and leaned against her father's arm. For months she had looked forward to the baby coming, and now to be told there would be no little one to wheel around in the perambulator! The shock was just too much.

"Tomorrow, my little flower." Charles kissed the top of his daughter's head. "Let Mama sleep tonight."

CHAPTER 5

Lily looked down at her useless skinny legs as she sat on the chair; the legs that used to run for miles over the downs, but now could not even get her out of bed without help. The skin on her shins was thin and hairless, and Matron had placed a large dressing on the left shin where she knew an ulcer had formed.

Pamela must have come home by now. Why hadn't she been by? The days stretched endlessly one into the other. There was only the awful television set in the corner of the room blaring away to itself. If only there was something interesting to look at or listen to on it; Mr Logie Baird would be writhing in his grave today if he'd ever caught sight of the rubbish that was now called daytime TV.

Donna had helpfully left a beaker of tea and a biscuit. Lily reached out with her left arm, grabbed the beaker and put it to her lips. Ugh. It was cold. She must have fallen asleep and forgotten all about it. She nibbled the biscuit instead, but it was too dry without any liquid. With a shudder she sipped the cold tea to wash it down. At least there was some sugar in it though.

"Here's your lunch. I've cut it all up for you." Donna removed the beaker of cold tea, replaced it with some water, and put a bowl of chicken and pasta with tomato sauce in front of Lily on a tray. She put a spoon in Lily's left hand.

"Eat up Lily. I want to see it all gone when I come back in! We've got a new lady next door now, and I've got to take her some lunch too."

"Heshhhhh……er…." Donna had disappeared before Lily had a chance to stutter out her thanks.

***

The pasta was nice and hot. Lily slowly put some onto the spoon and put it in her mouth. The sauce was rather spicy though, and not to her taste. She pushed the spoon around the bowl again, trying to trap a piece of chicken. If only the right hand would work; trying to eat with the wrong hand took all her concentration, and she knew the food would be cold long before she could finish it up. After a while, the effort of chewing made Lily feel sleepy. Her head sunk down onto her chest:

"Come on Mrs Read, finish up your dinner."

Oh no, it was the horrible one back again. Lily looked at her plate. She'd eaten most of it and was full up.

"Isss……." Lily tried to say that she couldn't eat another thing.

"Open your mouth!" Bridie impatiently pushed some of the cold pasta in.

What could a body do that didn't want any more dinner? Lily could only come up with one answer. She spat it out.

Bridie's hands were uncaring as she placed Lily on the commode.

"If you think I'm sitting here all day feeding you, you can think again!" She placed the back of Lily's dress over the backrest of the commode, thus rendering her immobile, and took away the plate.

"You'll get no more dinner now!"

Lily smiled to herself. *Victory! A small one, but a victory nonetheless.*

CHAPTER 6

"Can I help you Mama?"

Evelyn smiled at Lily as she lowered the wooden clothes drier that hung above the range. Her daughter was going to make somebody a perfect wife:

"Please could you find Violet? She told me she would be painting out in the garden, but I've looked out of the window and I can't see her. I need to take her up to the Hall to meet Cook."

"Of course, Mama. I'll find her and tell her to come home."

Lily felt slightly annoyed at having to go and find her sister on her afternoon off. Violet knew she shouldn't wander about in the grounds of Bedbury Hall, but she had probably sneaked in to either pick the daffodils or to paint them, and was so dreamy and scatterbrained that she'd probably forgotten she should not be in there. Lily remembered Mama telling her some while ago that fourteen-year-old Violet was a bit 'other-wordly'. Now that Daisy and Leonard were married and were teachers at Freshwater school, Lily knew it was down to her to help Mama and keep an eye on her sister.

***

After a quick check around the garden, Lily strolled out into the grounds of the Hall. Birdsong filled the air, and she was tempted to go and find her father on the other side of the walled garden. However, she knew Lord Henry would frown upon this, and so she walked on stoically until she came across her sister's easel down by the stream, just exactly where she knew it would be. However, Violet was nowhere to be seen.

Approaching the easel, Lily could see the watercolours were still wet on the painting. Violet truly did have a gift from God; the daffodils waving their yellow trumpets by the stream that she had painted looked exactly like the view that was in front of Lily as she stood there by the easel. But where was her sister?

The afternoon sun was warm on Lily's back. She swivelled her head from left to right, swatting a fly as it flew too close to her face. She looked towards the icehouse on the opposite side of the stream, and thought she saw a flash of movement inside.

Lily skipped over the wooden bridge and on towards the icehouse:

"Violet! Are you in there? Mama says to come home now!" She carried on to the entrance and popped her head inside. The cool air was a direct contrast to the beautiful Spring day outside.

Violet sat on the floor sobbing, half propped up against the wall:

"What's the matter? Why are you crying?" Lily sat with her sister and gave her a hug. "You know you're not allowed in here. Come on, tell me. I won't tell Mama."

Violet shook her head, stood up and smoothed down her skirts. She stood up with difficulty, wiped her eyes, and walked back to her easel without saying a word. Lily helped her to pack up. She took a few sideways glances at her sister's downcast face as they walked home, but Violet was giving nothing away.

Lily soon overheard her parents talking about the sudden difference in their youngest daughter:

"Violet is uncharacteristically silent, Charles. She's hardly moving from the house except to go to work." Evelyn's voice sounded worried.

"Have you asked her if there's anything wrong?" Charles usually left the girls' welfare to his wife to deal with.

"Of course; but she just shakes her head and looks down on the ground."

Lily noticed how instantly her father was concerned for Violet's well-being, as he sought to comfort his wife.

"I'll do some painting with her on Sunday and see if I can do any better."

CHAPTER 7

Lily sat naked on the chair, dripping wet. Donna was careful, but Lily still did not like being washed. She remembered being scrubbed with Lifebuoy soap and her mother's rough hands whilst sitting in a tin bath in front of an open fire every Friday evening. Her father would have gone down to the Red Lion Inn to let all his womenfolk bathe in peace, and her mother would have taken great care to make sure that all three girls washed properly, scrubbing anything that had been missed. Lily could still hear Violet's protestations that she had washed absolutely everything, and her mother confidently assuring her that actually she had not.

"Come on, I'll take you back to your room now."

Donna expertly lifted Lily, now dried, powdered and dressed, and moved her into a wheelchair. On the way back to her room Lily noticed that somebody was now occupying the bedroom next to hers that had been empty for some time.

"There's a new lady in there now, Lily. Everyone calls her 'Robbo'. I think she's a bit shy though. When she's settled in a bit more I'll bring her in to meet you."

Donna settled Lily back in her armchair and turned on the television.

"There you go, there's something for you to watch." Donna headed for the door. "I've got to help Robbo with her shower now."

"Thuss…….." Lily sighed. *She had tried to tell Donna that she did not want that infernal piece of machinery turned on again, but the words refused to come out properly. She could not even attempt to think her own thoughts over the noise of it.*

Lily closed her eyes. The hot shower had made her feel tired. The banal conversations of the television presenters faded away as sleep overcame her.

A familiar voice jolted her awake. She had no idea how long she'd been asleep:

"Mum, it's Edward." A solid warm hand caught hold of hers.

Lily opened her eyes. *Dear Edward. He'd come all this way to see her!* She squeezed his hand. Her eyes glittered with tears.

"Gshhh…"

"Don't try and talk. I'm here for a few days to research a new book. I'll come and see you every day and help you with your lunch. It's just arrived now."

Edward took the proffered tray of sandwiches and cake from Donna, and cut the bread up into more biteable sizes. The sandwiches were delicious, and Lily gazed happily at Edward as she ate. She'd always felt a special bond with this one; growing up he'd reminded her of Violet; day-dreamy and arty. There'd never been a cross word spoken between them.

"Pam's not well today, Mum. She sends her love, but she's got a cold." Edward lied easily as he cut some cake and put the plate in front of his mother. Lily took a piece of the jam sponge and thought that all her birthdays had come at once; her favourite son and her favourite cake all on the same day.

Chewing was such hard work. Lily felt her eyes getting heavy again soon after she'd finished eating, but when she woke up again Edward was still there holding her hand.

CHAPTER 8

"Have you not needed to use any monthly rags, Violet?"

Evelyn was not aware that Lily could hear them both talking in the next room, as she got herself ready for work.

"I haven't needed any this month or last month." Violet was lying on her bed, unwilling to get up for her new post as kitchen maid at the Hall.

"Are you ill today? Why are you still in bed?"

Lily knew her parents were still terribly worried about Violet. Her father had not managed to glean any information at all during their drawing and painting sessions.

"I've been sick twice this morning. Usually it's been just once lately, but it was twice today and I really don't feel like getting up. I'm sorry Mama." Violet turned over in bed towards the wall and away from her mother. "Please let me sleep."

Evelyn sighed and left the bedroom.

"What's wrong with Violet, Mama?"

Lily tied her apron behind her back. She enjoyed being a parlour maid at the Hall. It was just like helping her mother with the housework, but now she was getting paid for it. There was also her blossoming friendship with Arthur, the footman and messenger boy.

"We will let the doctor decide. I shall be taking her along there later on. The child is sickening for something." Evelyn could hardly bear to think about it. "Please tell Cook that Violet is sick."

With her sister ill, Lily knew that Cook would get her to wash the dirty pots and pans again. She had only just been promoted to parlour maid, but today was definitely going to be a backwards step. At that moment she wished she had been born clever like Daisy.

***

Cook was in a foul mood.

"There's twenty for lunch today, and no help from Violet! That child will never make a good kitchen maid. She's useless!" Cook spat the words out as she rolled the pastry out a little too energetically. "Lily, you will have to help me until your sister comes back."

By the end of the day Lily's back ached from stooping over the large enamel sink. She walked quickly back to the cottage and hoped Violet had got over whatever was ailing her.

However, there was nobody at home. Lily could see that some cold meat and bread had been left out for her. This was unheard of; Mama always had a meal prepared, and her father was always home by this time. She returned to the hallway, opened the front door and peered out, but not a soul was in sight.

Eating her cold supper, Lily then lit the lamps, drew the curtains, and waited for her family. Towards 9 o'clock there were sounds of voices at the front door:

"Mama! Papa! Where have you been?" Lily could see that Violet was with them. She had been crying. In fact Mama looked as if she had been crying too. Papa's face was as dark as thunder.

Evelyn took off her coat and hung it on the hallstand.

"Violet, you can go up to bed now."

"Yes Mama." Violet started up the stairs.

Lily followed her parents into the sitting room. Her father sank down into his armchair and put his head in his hands. Something had drained every last bit of colour from her mother's face.

"Is Violet well now, Mama? Can she go back to work tomorrow?" Lily started to panic at the scene in front of her.

"Violet will be going away. She will not be working at the Hall for a while until she's better."

"What's wrong with her?" Lily was distraught at the thought of losing her sister.

"She is ill. It's late now and we must all go to bed." Evelyn stood up and began to extinguish the lamps.

How Lily wished that she still shared a room with Daisy! Her sister would know what was going on. She would have to speak with her at the earliest opportunity. Arthur had invited her home for tea on their next afternoon off, but she could not even think of going there before she had spoken to Daisy.

CHAPTER 9

Lily closed her eyes and tried to pretend that Bridie was not there:

"You're a bold, bold woman Mrs Read!"

What on earth was she talking about? Lily didn't think she was brave at all. She was 92 and felt about as courageous as a new-born kitten....

"Swallow this." Lily could feel a tablet being pushed into her mouth and a cup being placed to her lips. "It will help your bowels to open. You're running a temperature. Your bowels haven't been opened for three days now."

"Gsh......" *Oh no, not a brown bomber! Why were they all so obsessed with the workings of her bowels?*

Lily sighed and kept her eyes shut. She had not a shred of dignity left any more. Her lack of bowel movements were being discussed loudly enough for all the other residents to hear. *Bette Davis had been correct when she'd complained that old age was not for sissies!*

With the tablet swallowed and Bridie's footsteps receding, Lily opened her eyes. Bridie had left a beaker of warm tea on the table, and had turned on the radio. *Why did these people think every waking hour had to be spent listening or watching something?* Lily liked to sit and remember and think of times gone by.

What had happened to Violet? Was her sister alive or dead? Some over-jolly presenter was talking to her as though she was five years old. If only she could reach over to where the radio was and shut him up.

She remembered the day when she'd found Violet crying in the ice-house. Her sister had never been the same after that. It was as though all the joy had gone out of her. Two months or so later she had disappeared off the face of the earth, and Lily had never seen her again. Mama and Papa would not mention her name, and it was as though she had never existed.

***

A pain shot through the small of her back, and Lily shifted uncomfortably in her armchair. If only she could stand up and move about, but those days were long gone now. If she tried to stand up it would only result in her being hauled unceremoniously off the floor and back into the armchair, and being shouted at into the bargain for even thinking of standing up in the first place.

A nasty gurgling sounded deep within her bowels. It would serve Bridie right if the laxative worked a little too well; it would be another small victory in the bigger battle to get even with that dreadful woman.

CHAPTER 10

Daisy ran the flat iron over one of the embroidered pillowcases that Lily had presented to her on her wedding day:

"They're still looking as good as new, even after a year. Look how well the colours have kept."

Lily folded the pillowcase and placed it on top of the pile of clean linen. She did not look forward to changing the topic of conversation:

"Do you know what's happened to Violet? Where's she gone? What's the matter with her? She hardly said a word to anybody before she went away!" Her voice was pleading and insistent as she looked towards her sister.

"I don't know. Mama wouldn't say." Daisy fixed her gaze upon the flat iron.

Lily thought she would burst if she did not immediately disclose the conversation she'd eavesdropped on between Cook and Janet, the Housekeeper:

"I've overheard talk at the Hall. They say she's going to have a child. How can that be? She's only 14 years' old!" Lily was stressed with the confusion of it all. "She's not married. How can you have a child if you're not married?"

"Lily, things have happened that we don't know about, or will ever know about." Daisy sighed and put the iron on the range to heat.

"You've been married a year. Why haven't you had a child? How do you get one?" Lily could not contain her curiosity any longer.

"It's something for Mama to tell you when you are to be married. Leonard and I cannot have children. Our children are the ones we teach." Daisy could not bring herself to tell her sister of such an unspeakable and horrific act.

"Did Mama tell you, then?" Lily realised that her mother would have known all along of course, as she had produced four babies.

"Yes, but only on the evening before my wedding." Daisy inwardly shuddered as she remembered the terror of her wedding night, Leonard's probing fingers, and the pain and shame of it all.

"Where's Violet? I miss her so much!" Lily could feel the tears starting to fall down her face.

"We must be patient until we see her again when she's recovered from whatever ails her."

Daisy came over to hug her sister. She was finding it easier and easier to deceive the gullible, innocent Lily.

"Can't I even write to her?" Lily sobbed into her sister's shoulder.

"You'll have to ask Mama if she knows Violet's address."

"She won't tell me."

"Then we shall have to wait until she comes back to us."

"Can you tell me about babies?" Lily pleaded, and watched her sister for a response.

Daisy kept her gaze on the pillowcase as she folded it:

"No, but I expect you will learn soon enough."

CHAPTER 11

The room stank. There was faeces everywhere; on her nightie, on the armchair, and all over the floor. It had just kept coming. Lily had pressed the nurse-call bell for a commode when her bowels could not hold on any more, but nobody had arrived. She sat terrified in her own excrement, afraid in case it was Bridie that would come in and see the mess. She closed her eyes and prayed for Donna when footsteps could eventually be heard in the passageway outside her bedroom door.

The smack to the side of her head made Lily feel a little dizzy.

"You've shit everywhere you disgusting old woman! Look at the state of you! Open your eyes and look at me!"

Lily was beyond terror. Her bladder discharged its contents involuntarily on hearing Bridie's rage, which only inflamed the situation even further:

"Sss……." Lily tried to say that she had not meant to soil herself. It was just that nobody had answered her call in time. She was mortified.

"What's going on in here?"

Lily's eyes opened at the sound of Matron's voice. *Saved!* She rubbed the side of her head slowly with her left hand.

"She does it on purpose, Matron."

Bridie's voice sounded almost sulky. She started to scrub the floor with disinfectant, and Lily noticed how the horrible one was wearing bright blue rubber gloves which seemed to stand out against the drabness of the brown bedroom carpet.

"I'll see you in my office Mrs Clinch when you've finished clearing up." Matron turned on her heel and disappeared downstairs.

***

Lily thought that maybe Bridie took a little more care than was usual in cleaning her up. She remained silent as she went about her duties, and when she was done she exited without a word. Some time later Matron gently shook her awake.

"Mrs Read. I have to ask you a question." Matron was holding her hand.

Lily opened her eyes, momentarily confused. Where was she?

"Mrs Read. Can you hear me? Were you hit by Nurse Clinch? Squeeze my hand if she hit you."

Lily squeezed as hard as she could.

"You've just confirmed my suspicions. Thank you. I'm dispensing with her services. You won't have to see her again."

If she could have stood up unaided, Lily would have done a little dance around the room.

CHAPTER 12

"Mother, this is Lily."

"Come in dear! Pleased to meet you!" Bertha Read smiled and extended a plump hand.

Lily was nervous, and terrified of making a mistake. However, Bertha had a knack of putting people at ease, and soon they were chatting like old friends.

"Artie's father Bill was killed in the first Boer war. I've had to bring Artie and his younger brother George up myself these past years. George works for Farmer Dewsbury and I cook and clean at the farmhouse, so between us we manage ok. Where do you live, dear?"

Bertha set out a slab of homemade fruit cake, and some scones and jam on the parlour table for tea.

"With my parents in a tied cottage on Lord Bedbury's estate. My father is the head gardener there."

Arthur sat in his father's old armchair and rested his hands on the pretty embroidered antimacassars:

"Lily's a parlour maid for Lord Bedbury, Mother."

"You're not afraid of hard work then, I can see that!" Bertha looked on at Lily approvingly, as she helped to carry the tea cups into the parlour.

"My mother always says that hard work doesn't kill anybody."

"She's right. Come and sit at the table, Artie, and have some tea."

***

The parlour was neat and tidy and had a nice homely feel to it. Lily hoped she was making a good impression as she nibbled politely on a scone. She was glad she had put on her smart blue cotton dress with the velvet trim. However, her new boots were too tight, and she shuffled her feet uncomfortably under the table.

"Have you any sisters or brothers, Lily?" Bertha smiled as she passed around the plate of scones.

"My sister Daisy is married now, so there's just me at home." Lily found it reassuring that Artie did not seem to have mentioned anything to Bertha regarding Violet.

"You're a big help to your mother I'll bet." Bertha spooned some jam onto her plate.

"I try to be. I'm not clever like Daisy though."

"Clever is as clever does, my girl."

What did she mean? Lily looked questioningly at Artie, but he shrugged his shoulders and continued eating.

"This is lovely cake. Would you consider sharing the recipe?"

Lily knew her mother's cake tasted better, but Bertha appeared suitably flattered:

"Of course! The recipe has been handed down for generations – on my side of course, not on Bill's."

Lily smiled and ate cake until she felt full enough to burst, but all in all when it came to five o'clock she felt that the little tea party had gone rather well. She helped Bertha to clear the plates while Artie read the evening newspaper.

***

The following day at work Lily saw Artie as she walked past the backstairs lobby on her way to the kitchens.

"My mother likes you. She told me." Arthur smiled and looked up from his boot-cleaning duties.

"She's nice. I like her too." Lily rested a heavy tray on one hip.

"Are you off duty on Saturday evening?"

"Yes, I think so."

"Can I call for you?"

"Yes. You'll be able to meet my mother and father."

"I'll better wear my best suit then!"

Saturday evening came around finally. The Grandfather clock ticked loudly as Lily and Arthur sat together after tea in the parlour on Evelyn's best sofa. Evelyn and Charles had discreetly removed themselves to the sitting room. Arthur's heart began to race as he began the conversation he'd been practising all week

"Billy's been promoted to Head Footman, and I've been asked to fill the First Footman post." .

"You're going to be promoted to First Footman? Congratulations!" Lily smiled and tried to think of something else to say.

"Well I haven't agreed yet, because if I take up the post I'll have to stay unwed."

"Do you think you'll take it then?" Lily felt a sudden excitement at what the conversation might be leading up to.

"Only if you say no."

"To what?"

Arthur stood up and then bent down on one knee and took Lily's hand in his.

"Lily, will you marry me?" He was breathless, waiting for an answer from the girl he loved more than anyone else in the world. "There's no-one else for me, but you."

Lily didn't have to think too long. Artie was a good man, solid and reliable. She loved him.

"Yes Artie, of course I'll marry you!"

Arthur kissed her hand with relief.

"Thank you Lil! You've made me the happiest man in the world! Mother will be so pleased!"

"What will you do about the promotion then?"

"We can't both work at the Hall if we're married. George says there's work for me on the farm. You stay at the Hall with Lord Bedbury, and I can work for Farmer Dewsbury. There's an empty cottage that we might be able to have that belongs to the farm, just along the Causeway by the estuary. I love you, Lily."

"I love you too." Lily closed her eyes as she felt Arthur's lips brush hers. "We must go and tell Mama and Papa the good news."

CHAPTER 13

Even Donna was happier than she'd ever been (if that was possible) now that Bridie had gone, and Lily no longer dreaded the sound of footsteps outside in the passage. A sweet girl, Amber, had taken Bridie's place, and Lily felt that perhaps the rest of her meagre life would be worth living after all.

"Your daughter's here!" Amber stopped the trolley outside the room and brought Lily a beaker of warm tea and a shortbread biscuit. 'Would you like a cup of tea Mrs Newman?"

"Not at the moment. I'm fine, but thanks for asking."

Lily turned her head. *That voice wasn't Pamela's. Goodness gracious, it was Emily!*

"Hheeee….."

"Don't try and talk, Mum."

Emily Newman kissed her mother and wondered whether she ought to break the bad news. Edward had told her not to, but her mother was compos mentis and she ought to know.

"I'm staying with Pam for a few days. She hasn't been well."

Lily knew that. Edward had already told her. *Why did she need her sister to come over and stay just because she had a chill?*

"She's been diagnosed with breast cancer, and she's had an operation to remove her left breast. When she's recovered she's got to have chemotherapy."

Not Pam! Not her youngest baby! No! Lily's arm reached out for Emily. Her eyes blurred with tears. Emily held her mother's hand.

"Don't cry, Mum. It was at the first stage, and the doctors think they've got all of it. She's going to be fine after the chemo. She says she's sorry but she can't come in and see you at the moment."

"Isss…" Lily struggled to speak.

It was she, Lily, who should be looking after Pam, not Emily. Hadn't she always looked after her? It was her duty as a mother. And where was Pam's no-good husband this time? Oh, if only she could get off the chair by herself.….

"Drink your tea. It's getting cold." Emily lifted the beaker to Lily's lips and broke the biscuit in half. "Don't worry. Pam's home now and she's recovering."

***

The shock waves from Emily's disclosure had not gone away by the evening. Lily could not seem to eat much dinner despite Amber's coaxing. To cheer her up, Amber took the plate away and came back in with an elderly lady on her arm.

"Lily, this is Robbo, who's in the room next door to you. She's been wanting to say hello to you for a long time, so I brought her in."

Robbo had a stooped-forward, humped posture. Lily thought she probably had osteoporosis, and she remembered how her grandmother had also adopted a similar posture in old age.

"Hello Lily." Robbo's voice was soft and quavery.

"Lily can't speak." Amber brought Robbo a bit nearer as Lily held out her hand. "She's saying how do you do, Robbo!"

"I know."

Robbo shook Lily's outstretched hand, and the two old ladies smiled at each other.

CHAPTER 14

"Will it be finished soon, Mama?" Lily stood impatiently as Evelyn adjusted the hem of her wedding dress.

"I've just got to sew the hem now that you're wearing the right shoes. It will be done by the end of the week."

"There's only two weeks to go now!"

Lily's excitement was tinged with sadness, as she knew she would be leaving her parents to start married life in the rented farm cottage near to the church where she and Artie were due to be married.

"It's a good time now I think to tell you about what will happen on your wedding night." Evelyn placed another pin in the hem. "Turn around a little bit Lily please."

Lily changed position and prepared to listen with interest. Daisy had mentioned that their mother had told her the self-same thing on the day before she and Leonard were due to be married.

"What will happen Mama?"

"Well, Arthur will want to show his love for you."

"How?"

"He will want to show his love for your body. Gentlemen like Arthur will wait until they are married before they do this. However, some men do not want to wait."

"Artie hasn't said anything to me about this yet."

"Then he is a true gentleman."

***

Evelyn pondered how to let her daughter down in the nicest possible way. Daisy had seemed terrified when she had learned.

"Arthur will want to see and touch your private places. He will also want you to touch his. His private place looks different from yours. I don't suppose you've ever seen a boy's private place, have you?"

Lily's face reddened with embarrassment. Her mother had only mentioned private places once when she was explaining about using the monthly rags.

"No, Mama. I don't know what one looks like."

Evelyn sighed.

"Arthur has a penis which will grow bigger when he sees your private places. It could grow bigger by several inches. He will want to put it inside your private place that is covered once a month by the rags when you have your bleed. If he does this at any time when you are not having a bleed, you might well become pregnant. If he does this while you are bleeding, then it is unlikely you will conceive."

Evelyn gave another sigh, pulled the hem straight, and thanked God the little talk was over. Lily was dumbfounded. She'd had no idea. The whole thing sounded horrible. She felt like crying.

"Does it hurt?" She could not imagine such a scenario.

"At first, but then usually the pain goes away on subsequent occasions. It's how babies are made. You need to know, and there is only me to tell you."

"How often will Artie want to do this?"

"Quite often at first I expect."

Evelyn finished pinning the hem. Lily was silent, trying to come to terms with what she'd just heard. She slipped the dress off her shoulders, and then had the most terrible thought.

"Is that what happened to Violet? Did a man do that to her? Cook said she was to have a child. Where is Violet, Mama?"

"Violet is dead."

Lily started to cry.

"She can't be dead! She's still a child! Why has there been no funeral? Where is she buried?"

"She is dead to me. Please do not ask about Violet again."

Evelyn stood up, turned on her heel, picked up the dress, and then walked out of the room without speaking another word.

CHAPTER 15

Lily turned to discover the source of the unfamiliar noise. It was Robbo, pushing her walking frame on wheels through the open door of her room.

"Hello Lily. I'm out for a little walk."

Lily was always pleased to see anybody coming through the door, especially now as she knew it would never be Bridie. She smiled at Robbo and held out her left arm.

"Lsshh….."

***

Robbo sat down with some difficulty in the visitor's chair.

"Thanks for asking me to stay. I have lots of aches and pains. I'm 90 now, and can't get about very well."

Lily could understand that. She had the same trouble. She nodded in sympathy and listened eagerly to her new friend.

"I'd been in the Whitcroft mental hospital near Newport almost since it opened in 1896. I was sent to a residential home a few years' ago when they eventually decided I was too old to be of any bother, but then when that also closed down I was sent here. I always told everyone that I was never mentally ill and never have been, but nobody ever believed me."

How awful. Lily could not even begin to imagine what the poor woman's life must have been like.

"The other residential home wasn't as nice as this one though. It's lovely to talk to people who don't shout at you! Anyway I'm going back now. I don't want to take up too much of your time. Can I come back again tomorrow?"

Lily nodded again. It was nice to have some company. She liked this lady.

It took Robbo a while to raise herself up from the chair. Her veined hands grabbed the walking frame for support, and she shuffled off slowly down the corridor. A few moments later Donna popped her head around the door.

"I saw Robbo in here a while ago. She's a nice lady, always eager for a chat." She moved Lily on to the commode and covered her legs with a blanket. "She's got no family to visit her, not like you, Lily. I'm sure the two of you are soon going to be good friends!"

Lily could not imagine having nobody at all coming to visit. All her children came to see her as often as they could, sometimes bringing the grandchildren with them as well. She and Artie had been blessed with three sons and three daughters, and her extended family seemed to be growing bigger every day.

"You've done a wee now. I'll lift you off the commode then." With one swift move Lily found herself back in her chair. She had no idea if she'd done a wee or not, but Donna seemed pleased. Sometimes she was aware of the need to wee, but other times there were embarrassing accidents that were getting more and more frequent.

"I'll be back later with some sandwiches for tea."

Lily smiled at Donna as she headed out the door. *Perhaps it wasn't going to be too bad living in the home now after all.*

CHAPTER 16

"I, Arthur William Read, take thee Lily Joan Roberts, to be my lawful wedded wife. To have and to hold from this day forward; for better, for worse, for richer, for poorer, in sickness and in health, to love and to cherish until death us do part, according to God's holy law. In the presence of God I make this vow."

Lily felt like a princess in her ankle length dress of pearl grey silk brocade. She was aware that Arthur could not take his eyes off her as he was speaking. She stood at the altar and repeated her vows to the congregation in a voice trembling with nervousness.

The minister smiled to try and help the bride relax.

"Lily, will you take Arthur to be your husband? Will you love him, comfort him, honour and protect him, and forsaking all others be faithful to him as long as you both shall live?"

"I will."

Lily smiled at Arthur, looking so handsome in his three-piece suit and cravat. She could not help but think ahead to the wedding night and what he might look like once he had taken off the suit, especially the trousers. She had no idea what a man's private place looked like. She was terrified.

Arthur placed the wedding ring on the third finger of Lily's left hand.

"Lily, I give you this ring as a sign of our marriage. With my body I honour you, all that I am I give to you, and all that I have I share with you within the love of God, Father, Son, and Holy Spirit."

Lily looked down at the gold band. The minister was speaking, but she wasn't really listening. Before long she would be Artie's wife. She couldn't quite believe it.

"Those whom God hath joined together, let not man put asunder."

The minister joined their right hands together. She was suddenly a married woman at 17, able to have children. *Was she pregnant now?* She had no idea. She then had another scarier thought; *once the baby was in there – how did it come out?* She would have to ask her mother when the time came.

***

The bells of All Saints church were ringing the Quarter Peal as the wedding guests posed for an official photo, and afterwards filed into the village hall for tea, sandwiches and wedding cake. Arthur held on tightly to his new wife's hand as they mingled and chatted with their guests. All too soon the time came for them to say goodbye and walk the short journey down the Causeway to their little cottage that they had so lovingly furnished and prepared together. Arthur opened the door and then turned around to give Lily a shy smile:

"Can I carry you over the threshold, Lil?"

Arthur managed to close the door with his foot while still carrying Lily. She nestled her head into his shoulder. She closed her eyes briefly and wondered what on earth was going to happen to her next.

CHAPTER 17

How much time had gone past? Lily was losing track of the days. Meals were brought in to her and she was washed and dried and powdered, but for the life of her she had no idea what month it was, let alone which day.

"You've got a visitor, Lily!"

Amber popped her head round the door and woke Lily up as she snoozed in her chair. *Was it Robbo again?* She turned towards the door, but had to glance twice at her daughter before she recognised her. Pamela was much thinner, and wore a turban-like scarf on her head.

"Hello Mum!" Pamela gave Lily a kiss. "I'm sorry I haven't been by lately. I've had a course of chemotherapy and I've been rather sick. I'm on the mend now, but they say in time my hair will grow back."

Poor Pam. Lily held out her hand to her daughter. *She'd told her not to take that HRT. It could only bring trouble. Pam had said it was the best thing since sliced bread, but it wasn't right to interfere with nature. Once the change happened you had to accept it and find a way to deal with it that didn't involve popping pills full of hormones. If her husband had been any good he would have stayed and they could have found another way to deal with that tricky problem that probably most menopausal ladies suffered from. Yes, it was probably the reason why so many women in their fifties were divorced. She remembered though how Artie had been such a gentleman about the whole thing.........*

Pam held her mother's hand. It felt thin and frail. *How had her mother dealt with the terrible effects of the menopause? Why hadn't her father left to seek out a woman twenty years younger?* She would never know now, and when she could have asked she had not bothered, as she had not been suffering with the problem at the time.

"Love you, Mum."

Lily squeezed Pam's hand and smiled.

"Dorrie, Emily and Joe, and Alan can come over for your birthday, but Edward's in America at the moment at some book conference. We can have a little party in your room here."

"Wwwh…." Lily wanted to ask where Jack was, but could not manage to form the words properly. *Pamela had not even mentioned him. It was very strange.*

Was it her birthday?

Lily nodded her approval of the upcoming family gathering, but for the life of her she couldn't remember how old she was going to be. Perhaps one of the birthday cards would have her age written on it. Was she 91 now or 92? Would she be 92 or 93 on June 18th? Yes, she could still remember that she'd been born on June 18th 1880, so as far as she was concerned she couldn't be that far gone mentally. However, for the life of her she could not remember what year it was now.

"You're going to be 93, Mum. It'll be a big party!"

Ah, so it must be 1973 then. Lily made a mental note of the year. She made a resolution not to keep forgetting these things.

CHAPTER 18

Lily lay naked under the sheet with her new husband. She could hear the birds singing their dawn chorus outside. She had not been able to get to sleep properly.

She was a woman now. What her mother had left out were the emotions that accompany the sexual act. The declarations of love that Artie had whispered in the dark as he had laid his body on hers and the tenderness of his hands had caused all her fears to flee to a far off place, never to return. She hoped that Artie would want to make love to her again soon.

"Morning Lil! Are you ok?" What with working on a farm, Artie had got used to waking up early.

"Couldn't sleep thinking about you making love to me last night."

"It *was* special, wasn't it! Our first time together." He gave Lily a kiss. "I'm going to bring you breakfast in bed today. Make the most of it because I'm back at work on Monday."

"I love you Artie."

"I love you too, darling."

***

Arthur returned with boiled eggs, toast and cups of tea for them. They ate in bed companionably:

"You're spoiling me." Lily bit into a thick slice of buttery toast.

"Just for today, princess."

Breakfast eaten, they had no reason to get out of bed. Cuddling together, Lily pulled back the sheet and for the first time looked at her husband's naked body. The previous evening had been dark, but now she could see exactly what her mother had been talking about:

"I can't help it. It's the sight of you naked that does it!"

Arthur gazed with awe upon Lily's pale unblemished skin. She enjoyed his gaze upon her.

"Love me again, Artie. It's the most wonderful feeling." Arthur's lips touched hers, and the sound of the chattering birds in the garden began to fade away.

"At this rate we'll be parents before too long!" Arthur stroked Lily's hair as she lay on top of him, sleepy and sated.

"Mmm. I hope so." Lily sighed and nuzzled her face into her husband's warm chest. "How do the babies come out?"

"The same way that they go in, my darling."

"But......how?"

"Don't worry. You'll find out soon enough. Come along to the farm at lambing time and you'll get an idea!"

"No thanks. I don't want to think about it before I have to."

CHAPTER 19

Lily could not remember when so many of her children were all gathered together in the same place. Opposite her sat her eldest daughter Emily with husband Joe, and next to Joe was her daughter Dorothy and husband Ben. She looked around for Jack, but he was nowhere to be seen. Pamela and her third son Alan sat together laughing and remembering past family occasions:

"I remember when you pulled the legs off my doll. You were horrible to me!" Pamela seemed to Lily to have put on a little bit of weight. She looked a lot better.

"No, that was Edward! He blamed me for it!"

Alan chuckled and gave his sister a friendly punch. Lily thought that it was Alan who looked the most like Artie. *Yes, it was just like a younger Artie sitting in front of her*. It was uncanny.

"You all followed me around like ducklings. I could never go anywhere on my own!" Emily laughed. "I used to envy Jack. Off he would go with his friends, and I had all of you wherever I went!"

"You were so bossy, Em!" Dorothy started to mimic her elder sister. "Hold hands across the road. Edward - don't do that! Alan — leave Pamela alone!" Her impression caused even Lily to chuckle.

"See, I told you. You *were* always picking on me!" Pamela punched Alan in the shoulder.

"You were easy to wind up. Always have been." Alan smiled and looked towards the door as Amber brought in the cake. "Look Mum – the cake's here!"

Lily turned to see Amber carrying in a large iced birthday cake complete with two candles alight in the shape of a 9 and a 3:

"Happy birthday! Blow the candles out Lily and make a wish!"

Lily's eyes filled with tears. *She wished Artie were alive. She wished Pamela free from cancer. She wished Jack could have been with them today. She wished she could have known what had happened to Violet.* There were just too many wishes. She tried to blow the candles out, but age had made her too feeble.

"I'll help you, Mum." Emily blew hard on the candles as her brother and sisters clapped. "Now you're officially 93!" She took the knife that Amber had left and cut up the cake. "Mum – you're having the first bit."

The fruit cake was delicious. Lily was overwhelmed with the kindness of everyone.

"We're going to take you out in the wheelchair. It's a lovely day. We're going to wheel you around Freshwater so you can see how everything's still the same." Emily took charge of handing out small plates of cake.

"Still the same old Emily. Bossy as ever!" Alan ruffled his sister's hair affectionately.

CHAPTER 20

"Mama – the pain is terrible!" Lily paced backwards and forwards across the bedroom clutching the small of her back.

"Mrs Lacey's on her way. Is the pain down in your lower back?"

"Yes, right at the bottom. It's been like it for hours, but it's getting worse now."

Evelyn came over to where her daughter had stopped by the window, and started to massage her back:

"How's that? Any better?"

"A bit. Please don't leave me."

"I'm here Lily. I'll stay until after the baby's born."

Lily could hear Artie in the passageway downstairs talking to somebody. A few minutes later Mrs Lacey came upstairs. She felt Lily's abdomen.

"There's another pain coming, Lily. Try to relax and not tense up."

"I want Artie here with me!" She screamed as the pain tore through her body.

"Bringing a baby into the world is women's work. I've delivered enough babies over the past 30 years to know that this one won't be long in coming now."

Mrs Lacey spread a protective sheet and clean towels over the bed:

"Take off your clothes and put your nightshirt on, Lily." Evelyn helped her daughter to undress. 'Come and lie down on the towels. You need to get onto the bed now."

"I don't want to! I want Artie! I don't want this!" Lily screamed again in blind panic. She never imagined the pain would be this bad. Suddenly she felt as though she had to open her bowels:

"I need to go to outside to the privy! It's urgent!" She struggled to get off the bed.

"Stay there Lily! Just push as hard as you can! It's the baby coming! It gives you the same feeling as needing the privy!" Evelyn kneeled on the bed, with Mrs Lacey on the other side. "Hold our hands and open your knees. Push Lily, push for all you're worth!"

Lily sobbed and pushed with all her might. Her dinner came back up unexpectedly down her nightshirt with the next wave of pain.

"So sorry, Mama!" She tried to take off the sodden clothing, but the pain was all –consuming.

"Push again, Lily!" Evelyn thought of how much mess babies made coming into the world, and how much mess her daughter would have to clean up for years afterwards. *Daisy had the best idea; look after somebody else's children and give them back at the end of the day.*

"The head's out!" Mrs Lacey let go of Lily's hand to ease the baby's shoulders out through the birth canal.

"One more push Lily, and then you'll have your baby!"

Lily screamed again, gave an almighty push, and felt the baby slip out. She sank back on the bed, exhausted.

"It's a boy! A little boy!" He was already screaming in fury at being dragged from the warm, cosy womb. Mrs Lacey expertly cut the umbilical cord and washed the baby, then she massaged Lily's abdomen.

"The placenta will come out soon. It might help if you give a little cough."

Lily felt something slide out of her body, but she didn't want to look at it. Evelyn cleaned her daughter up and changed her nightshirt. The baby was presented to a happy mother wrapped in a clean white towel.

"Where's Artie?" Lily couldn't stop looking at the little life they had created. Mrs Lacey busied herself tidying the bed:

"We'll call him up in a minute when we've got everything spick and span. As I said before, this is women's work. No men allowed."

CHAPTER 21

The wheelchair jarred her spine somewhat, but Lily was delighted to see All Saints primary school again. There was a new front gate now that hadn't been there in the 1880's, and as they wheeled her along the side footpath she could see that building work over the years had made the school much bigger than she remembered, but she could still recall holding Violet's trembling hand on her first day and her sister's adamant refusal to step into the classroom.

"All right, Mum?" Pamela drew the knitted blanket higher over her mother's legs. Although it was summer she always seemed to feel cold.

Lily wiped away a tear and nodded as Pamela spoke again.

"Shall we carry on now up to the church and then to your old cottage?"

Lily nodded again and gave the school one last lingering glance. She remembered how Jack had loved his first day there, and had run off without even a backward glance.

***

Alan pushed the wheelchair up Hooke Hill. Lily could see the church still standing solidly against the elements at the top. She remembered when they'd built the lych gate in 1911. She smiled at Dorothy and Ben as they opened the gate, and pointed in the direction of her parents' graves. Alan steered the wheelchair around to the back of the churchyard to where Evelyn and Charles Roberts rested for eternity, side by side near the large stained glass window. To the right of her father's grave her gaze rested upon Artie's mother Bertha's headstone, and then Artie's grave next to it, all in a row. Her gaze noticed fresh flowers from the family propped up against Artie's tombstone. To the left of her mother's grave Lily saw poor Daisy's final resting place, and her baby brother's tiny headstone showing just the initials E.R and the date of March 10th 1888. Her mother had named him Edward. Lily sighed inwardly; the poor little soul had never stood a chance.

"Do you want to have a look inside the church?"

Lily nodded to Alan and as he wheeled her through the front door the musty smell and cool interior transported her back, and just for a moment she was a radiant 17-year-old bride again in her pearl grey brocade dress. She looked down the aisle towards the altar, but Artie was not there. She hung her head and closed her eyes.

***

The wheelchair rattled along the Causeway. The farm workers' cottage they had first shared was now transformed into a holiday home. It stood weathered and bowed opposite the now enlarged cottage that had once belonged to the level crossing keeper, his wife and their 11 children (*how on earth had they all lived together in just two rooms?*), where Artie had picked her up and carried her across the threshold, and had then closed the door to the rest of the world.

"Don't cry, Mum. Come on, we'll have a look at the bay."

Pamela signalled to Alan to leave. Lily realised she must have fallen asleep with the movement of the wheelchair, as she was awoken some time later by the sound of the waves crashing onto the shore. The family were sitting together on the shingle, talking in low voices and eating ice cream. Alan and Ben had obviously lifted her chair down onto the beach. She shivered, and felt cold in the stiff breeze.

"Would you like an ice cream?"

Lily shook her head. They were all being so kind, but she just wanted to go home. She turned her head towards the wooden seat on the small promenade where Artie used to sit, near to the shop. Once he'd retired he'd sit there every morning when he'd bought his newspaper, complete the crossword and watch the wind surfers. She'd always know where to find him. She closed her eyes and saw his face. He was smiling with love for her.

Lily woke up again with a start. The wheelchair was back on solid ground.

"We're just going to stop by Dad's seat."

She looked towards the shop to see if Artie was sitting nearby. *He wasn't there. Where was he then?* She looked around at the family. *He wasn't walking with them.* She began to panic.

"Wsssh…."

"It's ok Mum, we're just going to have a look at Dad's seat and then we'll go back."

***

As she came nearer to the seat Lily remembered why she could not see her Artie sitting there. However, what she had not seen there before was a bronze plate. She peered closer with interest.

"It's another birthday present for you, Mum." Alan wheeled her right up to the plate so that her eyes could focus on the inscription:

"Arthur William Read 1876 – 1967. Loving husband and father. He loved to sit here and watch the sea."

Lily raised her left hand backwards towards Alan. His hand was lovely and warm. She didn't know how to thank them all. He gave her fingers a little squeeze.

CHAPTER 22

Jack lay contentedly in his perambulator looking at the world around him as Lily pushed him towards her parents' cottage, where her mother had lunch ready. She had stopped breastfeeding three months' ago, but worryingly had soon started to suffer with the same symptoms that she'd had when she was first pregnant.

"I've not needed to use any rags for two months, Mama."

"Have you been sick?"

"Yes, many times." The sick feeling never seemed to go away.

"You are probably having another child, Lily. It can happen quite soon after you stop breastfeeding."

"But Jack's only nine months' old!"

"These things happen." Evelyn sighed and put down her knife and fork. "Men carry on living their lives the way they wish, and we have to pay the price."

Her mother sounded bitter and unhappy. Lily spooned mashed potato into Jack's mouth and decided it was no use fretting about an unwanted pregnancy; somehow or other she would have to cope with two babies when the time came. She would breastfeed the new baby for longer, and then deny Artie her loving embraces until each monthly bleed was just finishing. She was not sure what his reaction would be to this, but could not think of any other way to stop another baby coming so soon, as three babies to look after would be unthinkable.

"Daisy seemed troubled when she visited us on Sunday. She didn't even want to play with Jack." Lily had a feeling she might have discovered her sister's problem if Artie had been at work and she and Daisy had been on their own.

"Yes, I've noticed she's unhappy, but I'm not sure why."

Evelyn had already made an educated guess though. Daisy had been married for a few years, with no child to show for it.

"The school holidays will be starting soon. We'll have more time to talk." Lily laid Jack down in his pram for a nap. She felt nauseous after lunch, and on reaching home she just about managed to get to the privy in time. She sighed; her breasts felt swollen and sore. *Her mother was right: there was definitely another baby on the way.*

"We'll have to be careful after the new baby arrives. Three infants so close in age will be too much for me to cope with." Lily tried to break the bad news to Artie as gently as she could. "We will have to be intimate less often for a while."

"You're my wife, Lily. I don't want that to happen!" Arthur put down his evening newspaper. "I'll see if I can get hold of some condoms. We'll solve the problem that way."

CHAPTER 23

"Did you have a nice outing?"

Robbo put her head around the door of Lily's room. Lily smiled and nodded, and beckoned for her to enter. Even though she could not speak, she was pleased that Robbo seemed to enjoy her company. The old lady sat down slowly on the visitor's chair opposite. She sighed.

"You've got such a lovely family. I saw them taking you out the other day. I would have loved a family of my own but it wasn't to be. I was put in Whitcroft when I was 15 and that was it. I never left again for years."

Good God! Lily was shocked; Robbo seemed as sane as sane could be. *Why on earth had she been put in a mental institution?*

"Wshhh……."

"You probably want to know why, don't you?"

Lily nodded, and Robbo seemed wistful as she recalled the event:

"Well, I had a baby you see. I was 15 years old and I had a baby out of wedlock. I was forced to have sexual relations and I became pregnant. Nobody knew what to do with me. My parents disowned me. The baby was a girl, born on Tuesday 19th January 1897. I called her Mary Violet. She had lovely dark hair. I will remember that day for as long as I live. She was taken away from me and I never saw her again. I wonder where she is now and what sort of life she's had? She'd be about 76 now if she were still alive. I still think about her every day." Robbo looked sad and gazed down at the carpet.

Lily's eyes filled with tears and she reached her left hand out towards the old lady. *How could she have been treated so badly?* Robbo got to her feet with difficulty and took hold of Lily's hand.

"Don't you worry about me, I'm really happy here. I'm being treated well in my last years. I have a nice neighbour and it's lovely to be able to come in and see you. I'll come back again tomorrow." She walked slowly out of the room clutching her walking frame.

Lily remembered Violet. She had been 14 when she died. There had been the gossip at the Hall that she had been pregnant, so Lily had always wondered whether her sister had died in childbirth. Mama had never mentioned where Violet had been buried though, and a lifelong ambition of Lily's had always been to find the grave and pay her respects. However, she was too frail and weak now to continue her quest, so Violet's whereabouts would forever remain a mystery.

"Come on, Lily. Time for a wash and bed."

Donna gently removed Lily's clothing and filled a bowl full of hot water. Lily enjoyed the wash. She loved feeling fresh and clean.

CHAPTER 24

"Come in, Daisy. Jack's asleep for now and Artie's at the farm. We can have a nice chat."

Lily felt the baby squirming away inside her as she followed Daisy down the passageway into the kitchen.

"How long have you got to go now?"

Daisy made herself comfortable in a chair near to the range. It was a fair walk from Victoria Road to the Causeway, and she was glad to rest her legs.

"A few more weeks I think."

Lily sat down heavily in Artie's chair opposite her sister. "Mrs Lacey says the baby will be born at the end of February. I feel fit to burst."

Daisy fidgeted slightly in her chair.

"I can't have children." Her eyes filled with tears. "I can't have children because I can't have intimate relations with Leonard. I've never been able to undergo the sexual act at all."

She began to cry. Huge sobs emanated from her body at the release of years of pent-up emotions.

"Oh Daisy, I'm so sorry!"

Lily heaved herself up onto her feet and went over to her sister. Daisy stood and flung her arms around Lily.

"I think Leonard's tiring of me. I know he wants children. I love him but I can't bear him to touch me!"

Daisy couldn't seem to stop the tears. They flowed down her face and onto Lily's shoulder.

"Leonard loves you. Of course he's not tiring of you! Have you visited Dr Gould?"

"I couldn't possibly discuss my problem with a man. It's just too embarrassing. There doesn't seem to be any solution."

Daisy was at her wit's end, worried that Leonard was spending too many evenings at the Red Lion Inn, and convinced that he was seeing another woman. When her sobs had subsided into hiccups, she seated herself again and kept her gaze down on the floor.

Lily remained standing and put the kettle on the range to boil.

"Could you adopt?"

"Leonard doesn't want to. He wants our own children. I should never have married him." Daisy felt fresh tears welling behind her eyes. She wiped them away with a handkerchief. "How do you tolerate being so intimate?"

"I love Artie. I want him to make love to me." Lily gave a rueful laugh. "As you can see, we have the opposite problem of how to stop the babies coming!"

"The night before our wedding Mama explained what Leonard was going to do, and I was terrified." Daisy shuddered.

"Yes, I remember that conversation when I was to be wed. Mama gave me no indication that it might even be a little bit enjoyable!" Lily looked down at her huge stomach and couldn't bring herself to tell her sister of the many enjoyable hours she and Artie had passed exploring each other's bodies.

"What can I do, Lily?"

"If you want children you must have intimate relations. Perhaps just get used to Leonard touching you to start with?"

"I've tried that. I can't bear it."
"Then there's only one thing for it."
"What?" Daisy looked up with interest.
"Close your eyes and think of England."

CHAPTER 25

"Cooee – it's only me!" The sound of Robbo's voice woke Lily from her doze. She turned and held out her left hand in greeting.

"I didn't sleep well last night. I dozed off and dreamed I was back in Whitcroft. I was so relieved when I woke up and remembered I was here, that I couldn't get back to sleep again." Robbo briefly grasped Lily's hand before sitting herself down.

"I like coming in here to see you. I think of you like a sister. Once I had a sister called Lily, you know. Actually I had two sisters; the eldest one was called Daisy and the next one down was Lily. My real name is Violet. Mama used to call us her little flowers. When I was sent away I never saw my parents or either of my sisters again. There were two Violets at Whitcroft, so I was called by my surname of Roberts, which was shortened to Robbo soon after I got there."

Lily sat bolt upright, unbelieving.

"Essss…!" She cursed her body for its frailties. *This lady was Violet! Robbo was her sister! She had spent her whole life incarcerated in a mental institution just a few miles away from her family!*

"Lord Henry got away scot free with assaulting and raping me. He made sure I was shut away so I couldn't speak out against him."

Lily became agitated. *What could she do to alert Violet?* She suddenly remembered when the eldest of Emily's children had been born deaf. Emily and Joe had learned sign language, and to some extent the rest of the extended family had learned a few signs in order to communicate with Tommy. Lily could still remember the sign for 'sister'; she could still use her left arm.

She made the shape of a 'c' with the thumb and curved forefinger of her left hand. She tapped her nose with her forefinger for all she was worth.

"I don't understand sign language. What are you trying to say, Lily?" Violet appeared worried at her friend's distress.

Lily made a fist and punched her chest. Tears of happiness streamed from her eyes. She made another 'c' shape and tapped her nose again with her forefinger.

"Why are you crying Lily? What's the matter? I'll go and find one of the nurses!" Violet raised herself and shuffled out of the room clutching her walking frame.

A short time afterwards Amber came running up the stairs, followed a few moments later by Violet. Lily was still in tears.

"What's wrong?" Amber knelt down in front of Lily.

"Sss…!" Lily pointed towards Violet, punched her chest with her fist, made yet another 'c' sign, and tapped her nose again.

"Are you making the sign for sister, Lily? My brother is hard of hearing, and we've all learned signing at home."

Lily nodded. At last somebody understood her! She pointed towards Violet, punched her chest and tapped her nose.

"You're saying Robbo is your sister?"

Lily nodded and nodded until she thought her head might fall off. She looked around in wonder and saw Violet coming towards her. She held out her left hand. Violet took Lily's hand in hers and smiled.

"I knew it." Violet nodded. "I somehow knew that we were family. Don't ask me how I knew though, because I couldn't tell you. I'm so happy to have found you Lily!"

CHAPTER 26

"Who's that knocking at this time of night?" Arthur had been woken from a deep sleep. He grumbled as he opened the front door, but his expression changed when he saw his brother-in-law.

"Leonard! Come in out of the cold! Whatever's the matter?" Arthur could see that Leonard looked extremely worried.

"It's Daisy. She went out for a walk and hasn't come back. I've looked all over for her. I wondered if she was here by any chance?" Leonard looked past Arthur into the sitting room.

"No, she hasn't been by here today. Where did she say she was walking to?"

"She didn't, but she often goes up on High Down."

"It's dark now. We'll search on the downs for her at first light. What was she wearing when you last saw her?"

"A high necked white blouse, an ankle length blue skirt, and black button boots."

"We'll find her. Don't worry."

***

Lily padded downstairs, heavily pregnant, to find out what was going on:

"Daisy's missing. We'll be looking for her as soon as dawn breaks.

Can you make a bed up for Leonard please, Lily? He can sleep on the settee."

"Of course, but I'm sure she'll be back soon."

"It's not like her to be away from home in the evening. It's cold out there tonight." Leonard looked at the end of his tether. "I left her a note in case she returned home to say I was here."

By 7.15 the next morning Arthur and Leonard were dressed warmly and Lily had made them some hot porridge. She gave them both a kiss as they set off down the garden path.

"We'll check at home first, just in case she came back." Leonard turned to wave at Lily. "Thank you for putting me up last night."

"It was no trouble."

Lily could hear that Jack was awake in his cot. There was some porridge left over for him. She closed the front door and went upstairs to see to her son.

She would forever shudder on recalling Artie's pale face when he finally came home later that fateful afternoon. He had sat her down, put his arms around her, and dealt the blow as gently as he could.

***

It had taken them a good half an hour to walk back to Victoria Road. With no sign of Daisy at the house, he and Leonard had passed into Gate Lane, bade good day to Mr Orchard as he opened his grocery shop, and then walked onwards towards High Down through the early-morning mist. The air had been calm and still. It had been a beautiful morning. Cattle were grazing contentedly on the grassy hill leading up to the downs.

"Daisy loves it up here. She's always watching out for Lord Tennyson as she walks about." Leonard had spoken to Artie as he'd looked ahead and walked with purpose. He could see a man with a collie up ahead near the edge of the cliff.

"Have you seen a young woman walking up here recently with long auburn hair?" Leonard had shouted over to the man, who had cupped a hand to his ear. The man had then left the dog and started to walk towards Leonard and Artie. However, as he had walked nearer to them, the collie had begun to bark, causing the man to turn.

"What's the matter Timmy?" The man had whistled for the dog to come, but the collie had stood looking out to sea and barking for all he was worth.

'I'll be back in a moment", the man had shouted; "Timmy's seen something."

Artie and Leonard had watched as the man walked back to the collie and looked over the edge of the cliff. He then suddenly became agitated, had put the dog's lead back on, and had run quickly back towards High Down's entrance gate.

Leonard had then rushed over to the edge of the cliff, dropped onto his front and looked over the top. He had shouted for Artie on seeing somebody floating face down in the sea, being washed towards the shore with the incoming tide. Artie looked and had seen Daisy, drowned but still wearing her white blouse, long blue skirt, and black button boots. Her long chestnut ringlets were splayed out upon the water.

His stomach had regurgitated the porridge involuntarily. Leonard's screams could have probably been heard on the breeze all the way down into Freshwater Bay.

CHAPTER 27

"Here's a glass for you, Aunt Violet!" Pamela smiled as she handed out the flutes of champagne. "Time to celebrate! I've got an auntie I never knew I had, and the doctor says I'm doing fine!"

Violet took the glass with one hand, and held on to Lily's hand with the other.

"That's good news, Pamela. I just know you'll get well. As for me, I can't believe I've found my sister again after all these years! My old brain can't take it in." Violet smiled at Lily through her tears, "I don't want to let go of your hand, Lily, in case you go away."

Lily squeezed Violet's hand. She could not even go outside in the garden these days unless somebody took her, but right there in the room was where she wanted to stay anyway; next to Violet, her long-lost sister.

"Something to make me even happier than I am now would be to find my baby; my Mary, but I'll settle for this!" Violet took a sip of champagne and thought it seemed like all her birthdays had arrived on the same day.

"Amber says there's a double room empty here. Would the two of you like to share?" Pamela thought she probably knew the answer, but she would ask the question anyway.

"Of course! What do you think Lily?" Violet turned to look at

Lily, whose beaming smile had suddenly lit up the room. Lily nodded gratefully, squeezed Violet's hand, and sent a silent message of thanks up to the good Lord above.

"It'll be just like old times; you and me sharing a room like we did before Daisy left home."

Daisy. Poor Daisy. She should have been here to celebrate. Violet also seemed to share the same thoughts.

"I have the feeling that Daisy is no longer alive. Is that correct?" She decided it would be best not to mention the many times that Daisy had visited her at Whitcroft; happy smiling Daisy, free of any worries or cares.

Pamela nodded her head and glanced at Lily, who looked fixedly down at the pattern on the carpet.

"Aunt Daisy died when she was still a young woman. She was found floating face down in the sea at Freshwater Bay. Nobody knew how she died, whether it was an accident or suicide, but we think she probably jumped off the cliffs at Tennyson Down, or what you used to call High Down. She was always walking up there, looking for Lord Tennyson. Mum once told me she was very unhappy, although she didn't say why."

Only Lily and Leonard had known why Daisy had been so unhappy. Lily closed her eyes and thought back again to that terrible time. Leonard never really recovered, and went on to blame himself for his wife's death for the rest of his life. She sighed; if only there had been the amount of doctors and counsellors around then that there were today, then Daisy might still be alive.

CHAPTER 28

"God so loved the world that He gave His only son; that he who believes in Him may not perish but have eternal life."

The icy February winds blew around the many mourners standing by the grave. Lily was glad of her thick coat. She held onto Artie's hand and wept as Daisy's coffin was slowly lowered into the ground.

"For as much as it hath pleased the Lord to take the soul of Daisy Evelyn Roberts, we commit her body to the ground; earth to earth, ashes to ashes, dust to dust; in sure and certain hope of the Resurrection to eternal life."

Leonard stepped forward to throw a handful of earth onto the coffin, followed by Evelyn and Charles. Lily had kept silent about feeling twinges all morning, but suddenly could not ignore any longer the familiar deep contractions of childbirth, and was rooted to the spot in misery and pain. Daisy was gone forever, and she did not know how she was going to come to terms with that.

She looked at Jack, asleep against Artie's shoulder. Another spasm let her know that her son or daughter was impatient to make its entry into the world. She sighed; at least the new baby would be a welcome distraction from the dark days of mourning that were to come.

One by one the mourners filed out of the churchyard and across the road into the Red Lion Inn for sandwiches and a fortifying glass of sherry. Leonard sat down with a sigh in the nearest corner and closed his eyes. Charles sat next to his son-in-law and tried to offer support.

"Mama. The baby started coming early this morning. I have to get home." Lily looked at her mother's distraught face, and thought that probably the new birth might be the best thing to happen to the family at that precise moment.

"You go with Artie. I'll take Jack with me, and will go and find Mrs Lacey." Evelyn wiped away her tears, glad of something practical to do to stop her thinking about her dead daughter.

Lily found it terribly difficult to walk. The baby felt as though it might drop out at any minute. As she opened the front door her waters broke.

"Help me upstairs please Artie."

Lily was glad of her husband's help as she sat down heavily on the bed. This was not like the last time with Jack; her pains were coming too soon and too frequently. She started to panic at the late arrival of her mother and Mrs Lacey.

"Don't fret, Lil. I'm here."

"What if the baby comes before they get here?" Lily directed Arthur to put extra towels and sheeting on the bed, as she fought the urge to bear down.

"Then it'll come. I've delivered many lambs and calves on the farm. I'm sure it's not that different!" Arthur joked with a light-heartedness that he did not actually feel at that precise moment.

"It's coming, Artie. I can't stop it!" Lily took off her long black bombazine skirt, removed her bloomers and sat back against the headboard. The next pain took over her whole body, and the outside world faded into insignificance. Her only aim in life now was to push the baby out.

"Push Lily! Come on!" Artie tried to keep his voice from shaking with nervousness.

"I don't want to! Mama and Mrs Lacey aren't here!"

"I can see the head, Lily! Just push!"

Lily grabbed hold of her knees, put her head down and pushed with all her might. There was suddenly a wonderful release from all the pain.

"It's a girl. A little girl! We've got a daughter, Lil!"

The tears were real that were rolling down her husband's face. He wrapped the baby up in a towel before presenting Lily with her new daughter.

"Have you cut the cord?" Lily felt elated, and proud as punch of her husband.

"No. I'll leave that to Mrs Lacey. I can hear her outside now with Jack and your mother."

As he went downstairs to let them in, he stood in the doorway and turned towards Lily:

"From tomorrow onwards Mrs Lacey is retired. She's getting a bit past it now anyway. I'll watch her cut the cord and whatever else she has to do, and then I'm delivering the rest of our babies."

"But you can't, Artie! Men just don't do that!"

"This one does. It was wonderful. I wouldn't have missed it for the world! I love you, Lil."

"I love you too."

Lily smiled as she cuddled little Emily Daisy. Her husband really was the most remarkable man.

CHAPTER 29

"Mum. Are you awake?"

Lily opened her eyes. Pamela was definitely looking better, although she still wore the turban to cover her hair loss.

"We're going to try and find auntie Vi's daughter. We've had a little chat with her and she's given us all the information she could think of. It was Alan's idea. Isn't it great!"

How on earth would they be able to find her? Lily squeezed Pamela's hand and nodded. It was just like Alan to have come up with something so wonderful. Artie would definitely have done a similar thing. She looked at her sister opposite, sitting beaming in her bedside chair in the new twin room they now shared.

"We'll start by going along to Whitcroft and talking to somebody about letting us check through the old nursing records of 19th January 1897, and then we'll ask if we can look through auntie Vi's patient records. She's written a letter of authorisation agreeing that we can look through her notes. There must be some sort of record at the hospital of what happened that day. If there's nothing there, then we'll get onto the Council's adoption department to see what's in their archives. Alan says the County Council was formed in 1890, so there must be something written down saying where the baby went."

Lily's head spun with the news. Somewhere out there was a niece she had never met, living her life and probably quite unaware of the circumstances surrounding her birth.

Pamela bustled out, busy and on a mission. All thoughts of cancer had been put to the back of her mind. Lily thought the distraction could only do her the world of good.

"My Mary! I can't believe it, Lily!" Violet sighed and smiled over at her sister. "They're going to find my Mary!"

CHAPTER 30

"There's no conscription. Don't worry. I'm not going off to fight the Boers." Artie reached over to Lily, lying next to him in bed.

"I was just thinking of your father, that's all. I hoped against hope you didn't want to join the Army."

"Never! I want to be here with you and our children. I don't want to be thousands of miles away in South Africa."

"Thank God!" Lily kissed her husband and felt his warm, solid body. She loved him so much. She couldn't get enough of him.

Artie returned her kiss passionately. Lily wriggled underneath him and wrapped her legs around his back.

"Just let me get a rubber first." Artie reached over to the bedside table.

"No. Leave it. Let's make another baby!"

"Are you sure?"

"Positive! It's so much better making love without you having to put those things on."

"You're right there. It doesn't feel half as good either. It's like trying to thread a needle while I'm wearing mittens!" Artie laughed as he sat back to gaze at his wife's naked body. "You're beautiful, Lil. I want to make many babies with you."

"Well get on with it then!"

When the passion had died they lay together like two spoons, enjoying the silence and an easy familiarity.

"Do you think we've made another baby?" Lily kept her eyes closed, enjoying feeling the warmth of her husband's body as he lay on his side against her back.

"Well, I did my best." Artie held Lily tighter, feeling as though he never wanted to let her go.

"Arthur Read! What am I going to do with you?"

"I've got a few suggestions."

***

She did not remember dozing, but Emily's cries woke her suddenly. Artie still lay asleep against her back as Lily climbed out of bed and put on her nightshirt. The cold linoleum of the passageway was unpleasant on her bare feet. She lit a candle and shivering, yawned her way to the children's bedroom. She wondered when on earth her two-year-old daughter would begin sleeping through the night.

"Hush. Hush. Mummy's here."

Lily stroked her daughter's blonde curls and settled her down again. The candlelight cast flickering shadows on Emily's perfect baby face. In the far corner of the room three-and-a-half-year-old Jack had finally put down his tin soldiers and was deeply asleep.

Lily sighed contentedly. Her husband and children were her life. All was well in her little world.

As time went on it became apparent to Lily that they had indeed made another baby. By the time Dorothy had made her quick entry into the world, Lily had begun to notice that although her mother was losing weight very quickly, her abdomen was terribly bloated. Evelyn seemed pale and listless, complained of constant diarrhoea, and could not find the energy or inclination to busy herself about the house or amuse her grandchildren when they came to visit. Charles had urged his wife to visit the doctor, but Evelyn did not want to waste any hard-earned money. She laid on the sofa and became a ghost of her former self, citing Daisy's death as the reason for her malaise.

CHAPTER 31

Violet and Lily listened intently to Pamela reading from her notes.

"They were very helpful at Whitcroft. They keep all their records in the basement. We went down and found the nursing notes detailing how Violet Roberts, 15, was delivered of a healthy baby girl at 11.15am on January 19th 1897. The baby was named Mary Violet and was given to the Benedictine nuns at St. Cecilia's Abbey for placement with adoptive parents."

"Oh Pamela. I can't thank you enough for what you're doing."

Pamela thought that the look on her aunt's face was thanks enough.

"I haven't finished yet auntie Vi. Alan and I then went to Ryde to speak to the nuns at the Abbey."

"Did you find anything?" Violet's voice was breathy with excitement.

"Yes." Pamela checked her notes once again. "Mary Roberts was placed with a Mr and Mrs Jacob Greensmith who at the time lived at 205 St. Thomas Street, Ryde. The trail's gone cold for the moment now. We think probably Mary's name might possibly have been changed to Greensmith. We'll make a trip to the Records Office to check on the Ryde parish registers to see if Mary was baptised, and maybe even check with the County Council."

Pamela saw the excitement on the old lady's face but did not want to give her false hope.

"It was a private adoption arrangement by the looks of it though, so I doubt the County Council will have any records, but the Records Office might if Mary was baptised or went to school on the island."

"Thank you so much. I'm weak and useless now, and I'm so sorry that I can't be of any help to you." Violet's lip quavered.

"Don't you worry about a thing; it's the least we can do for you." Pamela gave her aunt a kiss, and then reached over and took her mother's hand.

"I'll be back at the weekend. I'm going to Newport to make some enquiries. You two look after each other until I return." She kissed her mother, feeling the cold cheek against her lips. *Why were old people always cold?*

"Gggsssh………." Lily wanted to hug her daughter and tell her not to do too much.

"She says don't overdo it and make yourself ill." Violet smiled at her sister.

"Don't worry. I won't."

Pamela sailed out of the door, and Lily wondered how on earth Violet had known just what she was thinking.

CHAPTER 32

Evelyn's face was as pale as the white lace pillow, and her breath came in uneven rasps. Lily blocked the urge to cry in front of her mother, and concentrated on listening to her three children playing happily downstairs with their grandfather.

"Lily; I have to tell you something." Evelyn coughed and struggled to breathe.

"Don't fret. Save your strength." Lily was shocked at the speed in which the cancer had overtaken her mother.

"Hear me out. I need to go to my God with a clear conscience."

Evelyn's hands were warm as they rested on the counterpane. Lily noticed how big her mother's wedding ring seemed as she squeezed the thin fingers. *She would have to ask her father to tape it on to save it from becoming lost.*

"Edward was not stillborn. Do you hear me, Lily?" Evelyn closed her eyes with the effort of trying to speak.

"Of course he was! Whatever makes you think he wasn't?" Lily's heart started beating faster.

"The baby was born alive. I sent Mrs Lacey out. I pressed his face into my chest until he stopped breathing." Her mother's voice was just a whisper.

The ticking of the clock suddenly seemed very loud in the

bedroom. The coal fire spat and crackled, as Lily's mind whirled with her mother's revelations.

"Why? Why did you do it?" She could not keep the tears from running down her face.

"Didn't want it….. Already had three…." Evelyn lapsed into silence.

Lily felt the time was finally right to ask the one question that she'd been too afraid to mention for years. She took a deep breath.

"W-What happened to Violet?" She let go of her mother's hands and sobbed, remembering the little five-year-old girl skipping over High Down without a care in the world.

"She……"

Evelyn's breathing became erratic, and a rattle came from her throat. Her jaw loosened and became slack, and her grey eyes clouded over and gazed sightlessly towards the ceiling.

***

When the rattling had ceased, Lily pulled the sheet over her mother's dead face, dried her eyes, and felt the unborn baby quicken inside her for the first time; her fourth child. Her little brother had had the life snuffed out of him for the simple reason that his mother had not wanted a fourth child. There and then she decided that if her baby was a boy she was going to name him Edward.

CHAPTER 33

Every morning Lily would wake up and check that Violet had not been moved somewhere else in the night. Sometimes her sister was still asleep, and Lily would gaze at the old face on the pillow and try to reconcile it with the 14 year old girl who had set off so full of life on that fateful day to paint the daffodils at Bedbury Hall. One morning Violet was already awake and sitting up in bed smiling.

"Good morning sister. Yes, I'm still here. You needn't worry."

Lily thought it uncanny how Violet knew just what she was thinking. *How did she do that?*

"I saw things at Whitcroft, you know; dead people. After a few years it became normal for me to try and communicate with them. I saw Daisy many times and also our brother Edward, who grew up to be a tall handsome man. I've been given the gift of extra sensory perception. I think that's what they call it these days." Violet made her statement very matter-of-factly to her surprised sister before continuing.

"Edward told me he was born alive. Did you know that?"

Lily nodded.

"Daisy took her own life, but when she comes to me she is always happy and smiling. She raised Edward to manhood. He was the little boy she never had. They still visit me, you know. I still see them and

I see Papa too. I also have a spirit guide who is often with me." Violet smiled.

Astonished, Lily looked at her sister and considered herself very fortunate. She had always had her family of course, but now she also had Violet back who could seemingly communicate with the dead, and who somehow knew just what she was trying to say. Violet was the only one who could relay her feelings to the outside world. She had indeed been blessed with a psychic gift, and Lily was not about to let her sister's ability go to waste.

"Mmmh.."

"Mama?" Violet looked questioningly at Lily, who nodded.

"No I don't see Mama at all. The link with the spirit world works through love, and my love for Mama died on the day when she told me I'd brought shame on our family and must go away. Lord Henry wanted me out of the way too; I was an inconvenience to everybody. He paid for me to be shunted off to Whitcroft, and there I stayed; without my family and without my baby. It's funny though, but I've always felt my Mary is near to me, even though we've been apart all these years."

Lily saw tears in Violet's eyes and wanted to change the subject. However, Violet waved her worries aside.

"One day I know I'll see Mary again. I sometimes see three children with her; one of them no older than Edward. Poor Edward; he forgave Mama for her sins, but I never did."

Violet wiped her eyes with a handkerchief, swung her legs over the side of the bed, stood up shakily holding on to her walking frame, and shuffled off to the bathroom.

CHAPTER 34

By 1903, with Jack happily ensconced at All Saints school, Lily had her hands full with Emily, Dorothy and baby Edward. Artie worked long hours at the farm, but Lily found she enjoyed the interaction with her children and the chance she had been given to shape their little lives. She delighted on taking them out on nature walks, and patiently taught them the letters of the alphabet. Motherhood suited her, and the children thrived in her presence. Her mother-in-law and her father were always willing to help out with the grandchildren if they were free, and Lily found a great ally in Bertha.

"You're a natural born mother, Lily. Arthur's a very lucky man." Bertha picked up Edward, who was grizzling.

"He's cutting teeth. He's been out of sorts today. Thanks for stopping by." Lily helped Dorothy as the toddler tried to spoon-feed herself with some homemade soup. "I was never clever like Daisy though. I only ever wanted to be a wife and mother."

"It's the most important job in the world; don't you ever think otherwise." Bertha smiled at her daughter-in-law as she patted the baby's back. "I remember Daisy. She taught my nephew's children."

"Yes, I miss her every day." Lily wondered how much Bertha knew of the circumstances surrounding Daisy's death.

"Mrs Dewsbury mentioned once that you'd lost another sister a long time ago."

Lily looked at Bertha's face, trying to read her expression.

"Violet was ill, and died when she was fourteen."

"Oh. I'm sorry." There was a look of surprise on Bertha's face.

Lily thought it best to try and stem the gossip once and for all.

"Yes, she contracted TB. She was sent away to The Royal National Hospital at Ventnor, but they could not save her."

She had no idea where Violet was or if she was alive or dead, but she found it quite easy to lie. The explanation seemed utterly plausible, and thankfully her mother-in-law appeared satisfied.

"Terrible tragedy. Your poor mother must have been beside herself with grief."

"She never moved from the chair for weeks. She just sat staring into space. We even had to coax her to eat."

This part was true at least. Lily remembered her mother's decline which had only been arrested by the arrival of Jack, her first grandson.

"When Bill was killed in the first Boer war I didn't want to go on living, but I had to pull myself together for the sake of the two boys who were just babies at the time. Please God there won't be another war to take away our menfolk."

Lily admired the way in which her mother-in-law had managed to raise two sons unaided:

"You never remarried then?"

"No man would want a woman with two children by somebody else. I found work with the Dewsbury's and had help with the boys from my parents. We managed."

"You've done a fine job, Bertha."

"The work we women do is underrated and understated. The Government should pay us for the work we do in keeping the home fires burning."

"Ha ha! That'll be the day!" Lily gave a rueful laugh.

CHAPTER 35

"We're getting somewhere, Auntie Vi!"

Lily smiled at her daughter as she burst through the bedroom door waving a piece of paper. Pamela put on some spectacles and read from her notes.

"The Ryde parish registers at the Records Office show that Mary Violet Greensmith, born 19th January 1897 married a Peter Wyvern Daltrey on 6th March 1920. Her address is given as 205 St. Thomas Street, Ryde. That's our Mary!"

"Wwsssh…" Lily felt like crying.

"Yes it is wonderful news, Lily. I can hardly believe it! Now we know her name is Mary Daltrey. Thank you so much!" Violet took the piece of paper from Pamela's hand to scrutinise every word.

"I'm going to the council offices next to check on the register of electors. Her name might be on the electoral roll if she's still living on the island."

Lily felt that nothing was going to stop Pamela now she was starting to make headway. The idea that Violet could be reunited with her daughter again after more than 76 years seemed almost too good to be true. However, suddenly Lily had a terrible thought that she hoped Violet had not been able to pick up on:

What if Mary did not want to meet her birth mother?

She kept her face expressionless and turned her gaze towards Pamela. Violet did not need to know of such negative thoughts.

"If she would rather not meet me then at least she'll know we tried to find her, and I can be at peace with myself."

Lily wondered whether her sister had read her mind, or whether she had just come to the same conclusion herself. Either way, Violet's psychic abilities were uncanny.

"Cup of tea, ladies?" Amber stood in the doorway with the tea trolley.

"Yes please. Lovely." Violet took a cup for herself and Lily, but Pamela shook her head.

"I'm off to see a man now about an electoral roll."

"Good luck Pam, and thank you again." Violet looked up and smiled at her niece.

"My pleasure Auntie Vi. It's not every day I get to meet a cousin that I never knew I had."

CHAPTER 36

Lily looked sternly at the four little faces waiting impatiently to tuck in to the steaming chicken pie and vegetables in front of them on the table.

"Grandad will say grace first." She hissed.

Charles smiled at his grandchildren and squeezed Bertha's hand under the table.

"For what we are about to receive, may the Lord make us truly thankful."

"Amen." Replied Jack, Emily and Dorothy.

"Man." Said two-year-old Edward.

Lily hid a grin.

"Does anybody mind if I serve the children first?"

"Not at all. We can wait." Bertha Roberts smiled shyly at her new husband and returned the squeeze.

***

When the children were quietly eating, Lily passed around the pie plates and pots of vegetables. She could not help but notice how happy her father seemed these days; he had become a changed man since his marriage to Bertha. Lily was trying her best to reconcile the fact that her mother-in-law had now become her stepmother.

"Mrs Carr said how much she enjoyed the wedding. She said she especially enjoyed the roast beef sandwiches afterwards!"

"Thanks Artie and Lily for all your help, and I'll let George and Flossie know too." Bertha wondered how much of the wedding breakfast preparations her lazy youngest daughter in law had actually taken part in, and how much she had eventually decided to leave to George, Artie and Lily.

Lily suddenly felt nauseous and took only a small portion of pie.

"That wouldn't fill a bird up. Come on Lily, you're eating for two now." Artie looked over at his wife's plate.

"I'm always sick in the first few months, you know that."

"I was lucky. I didn't have one sick day with either of my two boys." Bertha's plate was piled high with vegetables.

"Your mother only felt ill when she was having you and Daisy."

Lily noticed how her father had omitted mentioning anything about Violet or Edward. She was disappointed in that her sister and brother seemed to have been forgotten about completely.

"Let's drink to the happy bride and groom!" Artie raised his glass of ale. "Come on children, pick up your beakers!"

Water began being spilt as the children joined in a little too enthusiastically.

"Here's to a long and happy life!"

Lily clinked her glass with her father's, and then helped Edward with the difficult task of keeping his beaker of water upright.

"Happy life!" Six year old Emily flashed a smile at her grandfather that melted his heart.

"Thank you, my darling. Your new grandmother has indeed made me a very happy man." Charles reached over to ruffle Emily's light brown curls.

"I wanted to marry Grandad." Four year old Dorothy looked close to tears.

"One day you'll find the right man to marry, my sweet." Charles laughed. "With your pretty face you'll have no shortage of beaus."

"Welcome to the family, Bertha." Lily nibbled on a piece of pastry and wondered how long it was going to stay down for.

"Thank you. I just want to say that no way would I ever want to take the place of your dear departed mother. Charles and I are agreed on this." Bertha looked ill at ease. "It just needed to be said straight away."

"Of course, but I'm just glad that the two of you have found happiness with each other. Please excuse me for a moment." Lily stood up, secure in the knowledge that she had favoured Bertha over her own mother for some time anyway.

She made as dignified an exit as she could from the room, and then ran to the outside privy. After expelling her stomach's contents she was surprised to find Artie waiting in the back garden for her:

"Alright old girl?" He took her in his arms and kissed the top of her head.

"I'm alright. It'll go. Don't worry." Lily sighed. "Let's get back to the others."

CHAPTER 37

"The doctor thinks you've suffered another stroke in the night, Lily. Don't fret. I'm here for you."

Lily was awake, but felt her body did not belong to her any more. She tried to move her left arm, but her brain's commands were not getting through to the affected limb. Somebody had turned her onto her right side, and she could see Violet was there sitting by the bed and holding her hand.

"You caused quite a little flurry earlier on. I've never seen so many people around your bed. I told them you'd be alright because I'd look after you."

Lily felt Violet squeezing her fingers, but could not grip her sister's hand in return.

"It's ok. Just lie there and rest. They say you can still swallow, so I'll be here to feed you."

Lily swallowed just to prove she could still do it, and felt another squeeze of her hand.

"Good. We'll manage, you and me."

***

What day was it? What year? Lily had no recollection. She could hear other voices in the room; one of them sounded like Pamela's.

"How is she, Donna?"

That was definitely Pamela's voice….

"As well as can be expected. She can still swallow. We've given her some porridge and she's just had a drink and a nice wash."

Porridge? A nice wash? Lily did not recall having either one. However, she could see that Violet was nodding her head.

"Yes you have had some breakfast. I sat here and helped you to eat."

Lily wondered if she was going mad. How could she have eaten porridge, drank something, had a wash, and then not remembered doing any of it? She wanted to cry.

"Mum, it's Pamela."

Of course it is! Did you think I'm so daft that I wouldn't recognise my own daughter?

"I've brought you some more roses. I know they're your favourites." Pamela fussed around, putting the flowers in a vase of water and setting it down by her mother's bed.

Lily took a deep breath as the roses' heady perfume filled the room.

"They're beautiful. She loves them." Violet smiled.

***

"When is your birthday, Auntie Vi?"

"8th October. Why?"

"Nothing. Just wanted to know. Not long to go then."

"Just a few weeks. I never thought I'd ever see 91."

"I'm *sure* I won't."

"Your father lived to 91. Your mother is 93. You've got a long life ahead of you."

"It's just that when you've had cancer, with every new pain you have you think it's all come back again." Pamela voiced her worst fear and rubbed her aching back.

"You've probably just pulled a muscle. Trust me. I know these things." Violet's voice was reassuring. "How did you get on with the council people?" "I'm about halfway through searching the island's electoral rolls for a Mary Daltrey, but I haven't found anything yet."

"I'm sure you will. I feel as though she's near me."

Lily listened to the voices around her and tried to move her arms and legs in the bed.

Nothing.

"Don't fret. Just rest. We're here."

Violet's voice lulled Lily back to a dreamless sleep.

CHAPTER 38

"It's a boy, Lily."

Artie expertly cut the cord and washed and dressed the baby, who protested in the only way he knew how. Lily gathered the screaming infant to her breast and the baby's cries stopped in an instant.

"You're a natural born mother. I love you Lil." Artie confidently set about the task of cleaning up after the birth of his fifth child.

"I love you too. We are so fortunate." Lily smiled, still energised from the relatively quick labour that had lasted only one hour and fifteen minutes.

"What shall we call him?" Artie wrapped the placenta in newspaper, ready for disposing in the outside earth closet.

Lily looked down at the baby suckling happily at her breast.

"I was thinking of either Alan or Alastair. What do you think?"

Artie came over and scrutinised his son's face:

"I think he looks like an Alan."

"Alan it is then." Lily lay back on the pillow and enjoyed the kind of total relaxation and relief that only usually follows childbirth.

"I'll give you a wash and change your nightshirt, and then we'll call Mum and the children in."

Lily let Artie lift the sleeping baby from her breast to place him in the crib that had also served his four brothers and sisters. She then took off her soiled nightshirt and enjoyed her husband's tender ministrations with the soap and hot sponge.

"You should do this for a living. You're better than Mrs Lacey ever was, God rest her soul."

"I do, but usually I'm delivering lambs instead of babies."

***

Feeling fresh and clean and wearing a pretty blue nightshirt, Lily signalled to Artie to open the bedroom door. Almost immediately she was surrounded by four excited children.

"Now, don't make too much noise. You'll wake the baby." Bertha supervised the children as they crowded around the crib.

"You have a baby brother." Lily smiled at her brood.

"What's his name, Mama?" Jack peered into the crib with interest.

"Alan; but you children can choose his middle name."

"Can it be John please?" Emily, already quite the little mother herself, looked quizzically at Lily.

"John is a good name." Lily nodded.

"My best friend at school is called Zachariah. Can he be called Zach?" Jack's voice sounded loudest over those of his sisters and brother.

"I don't think so, Jack. I think we're all agreed on Alan John." Artie ruffled his eldest son's hair. "Now let Mama rest for a few days and then she'll be as right as ninepence."

***

The fire crackled in the grate and Lily dozed, full to the brim with the hot vegetable broth lovingly prepared by her remarkable stepmother. She had been blessed with another sturdy little son. Fitting him into her daily routine would be no trouble at all.

CHAPTER 39

The autumn wind blew the leaves around outside the bedroom window. From her vantage point Lily watched them fluttering to the ground. She felt quite comfortable propped up against the pillows, and Violet was always nearby to straighten out the bedclothes.

"It's my birthday today, Lily. I'm 91. What do you think of that?"

Lily's eyes watched her sister traversing the room clutching her walking frame. *How could it be that she'd changed from being 14 years old to over 90 in an instant?*

"Breakfast time ladies!" Shirley, the new carer, plopped a tray in front of Lily containing a plate of porridge and a glass of orange juice.

"Keep mine warm, I'm going to feed Lily first." Violet sat herself down next to her sister.

"Are you sure? I'll feed her if you like." Shirley looked over at Violet.

"No. We're fine thanks. We'll manage like we always do."

Lily slowly swallowed the porridge, grateful for its sweetness and runny consistency. It seemed that Violet always knew how much to put on the spoon.

"You've got some visitors today ladies. Put your best frocks on." Shirley laughed as she put a hot plate over Violet's porridge. "I'll be along shortly to make Lily beautiful."

"She's already beautiful." Violet tut-tutted as she put more porridge on the spoon.

Had she ever been beautiful? Lily thought back. Daisy had been the brains of the family, but it was Violet who had been blessed with the good looks; the blue eyes and the flaxen hair that had obviously been irresistible as far as Lord Henry was concerned. She, Lily, had been the boring middle child, plain in looks and not really good at anything.

"You've got the love of your beautiful family; don't you ever forget that, Lily. I'd have given anything to have had your life." Violet brushed away a tear as she gazed at her sister.

Good looks fade, but Lily knew the love of her family had stayed constant throughout the years. Violet, as always, was correct. Perhaps just being a good wife and mother wasn't such a bad thing after all.

***

After her bed bath and resplendent in a new pale yellow dress, Lily gazed towards the door waiting for the visitors to arrive. She hoped they would get here before she felt the need to doze off again.

"Go to sleep if you want to. I'll give you a nudge when they get here." Violet held her hand and Lily closed her eyes.

"Happy birthday Auntie Vi. We have a big surprise for you!"

How long had she been asleep? Lily did not know, but suddenly the room was full of people. From her pillow she looked around and recognised Emily, Dorothy and Pamela, but there was also another elderly woman with them, slightly overweight, with greying permed hair and who was wearing a smart blue suit. Lily did not recognise the woman at all. She looked around at Violet, who had a look of disbelief on her face. There was a definite tension in the air:

"Mum and Auntie Vi, we've found Mary!" Pamela looked for a reaction from her mother and aunt, but they both looked at her with open mouths, stupefied.

"Hello Violet. I believe you're my birth mother."

Lily watched as Mary Daltrey stepped forward towards her sister. Violet stood up shakily, clutching her frame, and suddenly could find no words to speak. There were tears in both women's eyes as they hugged and cried. Emily, Dorothy and Pamela clapped and cheered, causing Shirley and Donna to come running in to see what all the noise was about.

"Mary! My Mary! I knew they'd find you!" Violet dried her eyes, took hold of her daughter's hand, and walked with her to Lily's bed.

"This is my sister Lily."

"So pleased to meet you!" Mary shook Lily's thin hand. "I never knew I had such a big family!" Mary sighed, sniffed, and blew her nose. "So many new people to get to know. They told me my mother had died in childbirth. That's why I never went looking for you." She hugged her mother again, and Violet beamed a smile big enough to light up the sky.

"This is the best birthday present I've ever had!"

Mary held on to her mother's hand:

"I'm a widow and had three children, but one died when he was a baby. I'm an artist and photographer. I'm happy to tell you that you also have two grandsons and one granddaughter. They're all grown up now and live on the mainland, but they can't wait to come and see you!"

Lily saw Violet sink down in her chair, exhausted by emotion. Once again she tried to move her arms to reach out to her sister, but found she was stuck fast to the bed by her frail and unyielding body.

CHAPTER 40

While her three eldest children were at school and Artie was at work on the farm, Lily enjoyed the days with her two infant sons. Edward was an absolute joy to her; quiet, sensitive and dreamy. He had learned all his letters by the age of three, and was starting to read simple words. Alan on the other hand was a more boisterous boy; running here and there, playing with Jack's discarded tin soldiers, and always wanting to climb trees on their nature walks.

Her children's appetites were insatiable. Lily began to keep hens in the back garden for a free supply of eggs. It was the elder children's duty to feed them when they came home from school, and to make sure they were safe in the henhouse at night away from the foxes. The Dewsbury family were good to Artie, and he and Lily always looked forward to the free joint of beef or pork that always came their way at Easter and Christmas.

Alan, the most like Artie in looks, grew into a noisy, headstrong child, and Lily started to dread him coming home from school. Within five minutes of entering the house he would have kicked Edward and made him cry, or might have stamped on Dorothy's doll or suchlike. His friends were all of a similar character, and Lily encouraged them all to play outside as much as possible in the good weather.

Lily looked at her eldest daughter and knew that one day Emily was going be a natural mother; she could always kept the youngest children in check, and Dorothy and Edward would follow their sister about like two little ducklings. Lily found Emily a great asset, missing her dreadfully when she was successful in obtaining employment as a parlour maid.

***

By the time Jack was in his teens the first rumblings of war were occurring, and with the assassination of Archduke Franz Ferdinand in June 1914, Lily was beside herself with worry. His days of playing with tin soldiers were behind him, and Jack was all for taking Lieutenant Colonel Rhodes' pound note and joining the 2nd battalion Isle of Wight Rifles. Lily together with Artie pleaded with their eldest son to re-consider, but to no avail. Jack and his friend Zachariah were two of the first young islander recruits to add a couple of years to their age and take the proffered pound.

On the day he was to leave for training at Parkhurst, Lily, heavily pregnant with her sixth child, put her arms around her son and drew him near to her.

"May the Lord watch over you and keep you."

"The war will only last a few weeks, Mama. Our battalion will be manning the forts here on the island. I'll be home in no time at all."

"God willing, son. God willing."

She stood back and let the tears fall. Her heart felt as though it would break. However, Jack was a man now, standing before her in in his khaki uniform, and nothing she could do or say would stop him from wanting to serve his country. *Thank goodness Artie was too old and the other boys were too young!* Lily watched her husband shake their son's hand, and with a hearty wave Jack lifted his backpack, turned, and walked down the garden path and off to war without even looking back.

The arrival of her last child, Pamela, took Lily's mind briefly from her eldest son, but Jack was usually always there in her thoughts. She looked forward to his letters, re-reading every line several times. Jack's training was continuing at Bury St. Edmunds, and she pointed out his new location on the map to the younger children.

On August 4th 1914 Britain declared war on Germany.

CHAPTER 41

Lily wondered whether past had started to mingle with the present. Jack and Daisy would appear in her dreams; they would be smiling and holding hands with Pam, Connie, and Mrs Lacey. Mary's face would come into focus, looking so much like 14-year old Violet that Lily would need to take a second glance. Was the face that of Mary or of one of her grandchildren?

All around her were children's voices; Emily chiding Alan and Jack, Dorothy crying, Pamela shouting, Mary's grandchildren chattering ten to the dozen to Violet, and Edward calling to her from the garden where he would be sitting with a book. Time lines merged and became one. Lily was unsure whether it was 1893 or 1973, but as she lay there listening to the sounds around her, she realised that it did not matter one iota; she had Violet back and that was all that mattered.

"Such a fine young man."

Her sister would often seem lost in another world, and Lily wondered if one of Mary's children or grandchildren had suddenly come to visit. With effort she turned her head on the pillow, but could see only the two of them in the room.

"He tells me he was one of the 250 soldiers in Princess Beatrice's Second Battalion Rifles, who joined up with the Fourth Hampshires and was then shipped off to Basra in 1916, fighting alongside the Indian Army."

Through half-closed eyes Lily could see her sister looking at her quizzically, but she decided to shut her lids and pretend to be asleep.

"He's no more than 16 or 17 and is wearing a black and green uniform with a wide belt and some sort of badge on his cap."

Lily wished that Violet would shut up. The memories of that awful time were buried deep within her, and now her sister was bringing them to the surface.

"He says he's your son, Lily. I'm getting the 'J' letter. It's Jack. He's telling me you've always blocked his death in your mind, but he wants you to come to terms with it and accept that he never came home from the war. He says you have to stop waiting for him to come back, because he's in a better place now."

Although she could not move hardly at all, the tears could still fall from her eyes. Lily sighed and let them soak into her pillow.

"He's telling me that he loves you. He says his father and grandfather are with him, but he says you must accept his death and let him go. He's quite insistent he cannot move on until you have done this. He's showing me the Vardar marshes north of Salonika where his body lies buried."

For nigh on 60 years Lily had held out the faint hope that Jack would miraculously reappear, but in the back of her mind she somehow knew that it was never going to happen. However, Violet had killed the last vestige of uncertainty, and at the ripe old age of 93 Lily realised it was time to mourn her son. She opened her eyes, looked at her sister through her tears, and nodded her head with difficulty.

"He thanks you a thousand times. He brings so much love to you, and gives you a single red poppy. He says to remember the good times."

How could Violet do this? Her gift was amazing. Lily moved her eyes around as much of the room as she could, but she could see no young man standing there wearing a green and black uniform. If only she could have seen her Jack even once more her life would have been complete.

"He says sometimes you've been able to smell cigarette smoke when nobody has been smoking in the room." Lily nodded as Violet carried on: "Well, it's just his way of being near you and letting you know that he's been around."

Lily thought back to the day long ago when she'd brought Jack into the world and how she'd screamed with the pain; but did the pain ever go? The raw pain of losing her child was just as real as the distant pangs of childbirth; and had taken her the best part of 57 years to come to terms with.

Lily reached out to Jack in her mind, imploring him to take her along with him, and was rewarded with a faint, almost imperceptible aroma of tobacco. She'd been shielded throughout the war in her little haven in Freshwater Bay; never really knowing just what her brave son and his comrades had endured in the mud-filled trenches.

"He's going now Lily. You've done the most wonderful thing that a mother could do for her son. He's free to move on now."

Lily felt her body become light, as light as air. Artie ran towards her, young, healthy, and laughing; he picked her up and twirled her around. She curled her arms and legs around him, her limbs responding in the quick, effortless way they had done when she had been a young woman. Together again they soared over Violet's head towards Jack and a far-off distant light, seeing Violet below looking up at them and smiling.

The End

If you have enjoyed this short story,
please consider leaving a review. Thank you.

You may also enjoy 'The Daughter-in-law Syndrome',
by Stevie Turner.